I0566342

his spy at night

book three, spy games series

PAULA
ALTENBURG

This book is a work of fiction. The characters, incidents, and dialogue are drawn from the author's imagination and are not real. Any resemblance to actual events or persons, living or dead, is entirely coincidental.

Published by Paula Altenburg
Stewiacke, Nova Scotia Canada
B0N 2J0

Copyright © 2016 by Paula Altenburg
Cover design by Syd Gill/Syd Gill Designs
Interior formatting by Author E.M.S.
Edited by Nancy Cassidy/The Red Pen Coach

ISBN: 978-0-9937166-4-5
www.paulaaltenburg.com

All Rights Reserved

Printed in the U.S.A.

"International intrigue, adversaries with more in common than they want to admit, and ohhhh the chemistry…I couldn't put Her Spy To Have down!" ~Samanthe Beck, *USA Today* Bestselling Author of *Emergency Engagement*

He'd begin a game of his own. His would be more direct. She could use the reminder that, if she planned to pursue men like Vanderloord, at least one of her boundaries should be inflexible. Sympathy was about to become her mistake. She believed him trustworthy.

Well, he was a man too.

He slung an elbow over the back of his seat, allowing the knuckles of his dangling fingers to gently stroke the smooth skin of her naked upper arm. His gaze dropped to her partially exposed breast, remained for a second, then flicked back to her face.

She went very still. Her eyes narrowed. "I didn't mean for you to practice on me."

They were sitting in his car on a side street in the hub of the city. Although it was late at night, and the street deserted, privacy was hardly assured. Nevertheless, he tossed down the gauntlet. "You can stop me anytime you like."

"Nobody's stopping you."

She sounded so complacent. So confident she'd best him. He almost relented. Instead, he tracked the tips of his fingers along the length of her shoulder to the base of her throat, then upward to her jaw. The pulse leaped beneath his light touch and he was glad he'd persisted. Some responses couldn't be feigned. He tucked the crook of his finger beneath her chin and angled it upward, bringing her mouth more in line with his. Seated, without the advantage of heels, she wasn't nearly as tall.

He bent forward, pressing his lips to hers. He eased his right hand behind her head and placed his left hand on her hip, tugging her body slightly toward him. If not for the stick shift and console between them, she'd be on his lap. He skimmed his hand lower to the top of her thigh, then beneath the whisper-thin fabric of her dress until his palm cupped bare flesh. He felt the sharp inhale of her breath, then caught its soft, fluttering release as she exhaled. Her arm slid beneath his jacket, curled around his waist, and her fingers dipped beneath the band of his trousers at the small of his back.

CHAPTER ONE

BEING CALLED INTO THE director's office wasn't how Marlies Wiersma had anticipated her Monday morning would begin.

On her lap perched the case file she'd been handed when she walked in the door and been told to take a seat. Lies wondered if she was about to be reprimanded, demoted or fired. That Dan, her team leader, had filed a report on her stung. She'd gone to him the minute she'd figured out she'd made a serious mistake and he'd thrown her under a bus in return. Deep down a part of her believed that if she'd been a man Dan would have kept her affair to himself.

The thought of crying in front of the CSIS director was too horrifying to contemplate. John Carmichael was retired military and a well-preserved sixty-three, if his assistant was to be believed, meaning he had plenty of experience in intelligence behind him. If he wanted to know how Lies felt about being broadsided this way, she planned to make him work for it. She held herself as steady as a living statue, refusing to give up any personal tells, keeping ramrod straight with her knees together and feet tucked neatly under her chair. She summoned her best

I don't give a damn smile. As soon as she got home that evening she could let it all out, but not before then.

"You can relax, Marlies," John said. "I know what you're thinking." Through the window beside his desk she could see the tops of the trees that lined the parking lot three stories below. He settled deeper into his chair and crossed one knee over the other, swinging the toe of his polished black leather loafer. Thoughtful gray eyes examined her, making it hard not to squirm. "You think Dan sold you out because you're a woman." She couldn't hold on to her smile any longer and her shift in expression must have made him think she was closer to tears than she was. "I was a team leader once, so yes, I know he could have kept this to himself." He gestured toward the file folder in her lap. "I asked him point blank if there was any reason you shouldn't be given this assignment and he told me about your affair with Michael Ajam. Then he said he didn't believe it would affect your ability to do your job. He had nothing but complimentary things to say about your professionalism."

A new assignment. Not a firing. She couldn't speak for fear she'd begin babbling her gratitude. She wasn't nearly as confident about her professionalism as she'd been a few weeks ago. At twenty-eight she'd been with CSIS for three years, but she'd only been in the field for a little more than three months, and getting involved with Michael had been a huge mistake straight out of the gate. She was young, she was blond, and she was pretty enough to catch most men's interest. She'd thought she was so smart too. She'd intended to use Michael as a way to get closer to the people he worked for. Instead, like a teenage girl, she'd fallen head over heels. She thanked every deity she could think of that she'd figured out he was far more experienced at this game than she was before she'd given anything away. He'd assumed she was a low-level bank teller who'd gotten cold feet after he'd asked her—on his boss's behalf—to make one too many wire transfers for him. Each of those transfers had been highly illegal, but small potatoes compared to what she'd really been looking for. He'd set her up, wanting to see what she would do with the information he fed her. As far as he'd ever know, she'd done nothing with it. She had that much satisfaction.

And now John and Dan were giving her a chance to redeem herself. Heady relief bolstered her resolve to do better next time. She'd learned her lesson.

"Thank you." She smoothed a palm over the file. "What's the assignment?"

John didn't answer straightaway, but gazed out the window, the lines around his eyes made more noticeable beneath a beam of bright morning sunlight. It was late summer in Ottawa and the day promised to be as hot and humid as the past eight had been. The city was experiencing a heat wave. *Thank you, climate change.*

"It's sensitive," he finally said, swiveling his attention—and his chair—back to her. "And for the most part unofficial. Any reports will come straight to me, not through Dan."

He proceeded to fill her in. Canada's aerospace and defense trade commissioner in the Netherlands had received intelligence suggesting a prominent businessman and Canadian ex-pat named Bernard Vanderloord was laundering money from the Middle East by filtering it through European Union defense contractors. Vanderloord had been a person of interest to CSIS for some time now. They knew he operated primarily out of the Netherlands, where he had dual citizenship. They'd also linked him to the theft of Canadian military weapons systems parts that had ended up in countries with nuclear capabilities that Canada didn't conduct military business with. CSIS also had reason to believe he had connections to the Russian Business Network, a known cybercrime organization. He was currently doing his best to get closer to Canada's defense trade commissioner because of an upcoming shipbuilding contract. The Dutch had an established shipbuilding industry that Canadian defense contractors, with less experience behind them, would like to tap into. Canadians were actively seeking strategic partners in the Netherlands through the current trade agreement between the two countries.

This was where Lies came in. Her parents were Dutch immigrants with family still in the Netherlands, and Lies spoke both Dutch and Frisian fluently. She knew the country well, having spent most summers with her cousins while growing up. And she'd just spent the past three months working on a money laundering case so she knew what to look for.

"We'd like you to go to the Netherlands, where you'd work in the trade commissioner's office as his personal assistant. We want you to get as close to Vanderloord as possible. He already knows Harry isn't much of a mark so he'll be looking for another way into the trade agreement."

Lies knew how fraud worked. If Vanderloord was a crime boss he'd either go for the top of the food chain or the bottom. Harry Jordan, the trade commissioner, sat at the top. Since Jordan wasn't willing to play Vanderloord's game, Lies would come in at a low-level position, someone new who hadn't yet formed any loyalties, and become a prime mark. Her pulse quickened. She'd assumed that, after her last failure, she'd be given insignificant assignments until she'd built up her team leader's confidence in her again. This, however…

This was her wheelhouse. She was equal parts thrilled and terrified. But last time, she'd gotten too close to her mark and the wound was still raw. While the Michael Ajam she'd fallen in love with had never existed, that didn't mean she wasn't mourning his loss. The real Michael, too, had an element of excitement inherent in him that she'd been drawn to. The criminal side to him had been the deal breaker however, and the fact that she'd misjudged him so completely tossed her confidence in herself to the wind.

"There's one more thing," John went on. "It's a big one. I want no one—and I mean not even Dan—to know what you discover. I'll be your team leader. We've already got enough on Vanderloord to put him out of commission. We aren't trying to do that. He and the Minister of National Defence are old friends. They went to university together. Intel we've received suggests Vanderloord and the minister are conducting business together. We want to find out how they're managing to keep it off the radar."

Lies couldn't believe what she was hearing. "To clarify—you aren't after Vanderloord. You really want to take down the Minister of National Defence?"

"I never liked him. His eyes are too close together."

It was an old and tired profiling joke but she was too stunned to appreciate that the director of CSIS had a dry sense of humor. Her last field assignment had ended in disaster. She'd hoped for a chance to redeem herself and this investigation would definitely do that, but botching it could ruin her career instead.

"You can do this, Marlies," John said, again reading her mind. His eyes sparkled with empathy. "Don't let one misstep throw you off your game. We've all been in your shoes. It's an occupational hazard to sometimes trust the wrong people. Trusting yourself is more important. Learn from it and move on."

"Of course I can do this," she said automatically, mentally crossing her fingers. Her job involved having to lie. If she couldn't convince John and Dan, and the trade commissioner, of her ability to get the work done, how could she expect to fool someone like Bernard Vanderloord? As far as liars went, he'd make Michael look like a student caught cheating on an entrance exam.

"Perfect." John reached for the phone on his desk. He lifted the receiver and punched a button on speed dial. "Can you send Harry in, please?" he said to his assistant.

Lies's ears perked up. Harry? As in Harry Jordan, the aerospace and defense trade commissioner who she was supposed to go to work for in the Netherlands?

Why was he in Ottawa?

Before she could speculate, or ask for clarification, the door cracked open behind her. She stood, gripping the file in her left hand as she turned to greet the man who'd be her boss for the foreseeable future.

Harry Jordan wasn't used to cooling his heels in an outer office, waiting on other people's schedules. Under normal circumstances people jumped to accommodate him—mostly because they wanted something only he could provide.

This time, however, he was the one seeking a favor, and John Carmichael had never been the type to cater to ego to begin with. That was one of the reasons they'd stayed friends over the years. So Harry was content to organize his thoughts and sip at the fresh cup of coffee he'd been handed. It wasn't as good as the Dutch brand he'd gotten spoiled on, but it was close.

The assistant hung up the phone.

"You can go in now, Mr. Jordan," she chirped. She was perky, personable and bright, and even though he was only thirty-six, she made Harry feel old and none of those things.

Nothing about CSIS made him comfortable. He hated intrigue and didn't like having to be here. If not for the complete faith he had in John as a human being, he probably wouldn't be. He'd have ignored the problem and hoped it went away.

That last part wasn't true. Harry might wish he could ignore it, but he'd have dealt with it somehow. Knowing John as a personal friend made for a much easier decision. Harry had come to Ottawa to discuss Bernard Vanderloord with him in person because he hadn't trusted the normal channels for passing on information.

It turned out he'd been right to be cautious. He was about to have an intelligence officer dumped on him, meaning he'd have to watch everything he said or did from now on because it would all end up with CSIS and then shared with God only knew who. The intelligence business worldwide relied on an exchange system. If he, or anyone else at the Canadian embassy, gave John's agent information that could be used to buy better intelligence from another organization, John wouldn't hesitate to exploit it.

A man couldn't trust anyone in this business, not even his friends, and it made Harry tired.

He left his empty coffee cup with the assistant and opened John's door.

A woman rose from the chair in front of the gleaming mahogany desk at the sound of Harry's entry and turned in a smooth, graceful motion to face him. She was tall and slender, with short blond ringlets and side-swept bangs that curled over one of her very direct, long-lashed blue eyes. She had the pale skin, rosy cheeks, and full red lips of the stereotypical Dutch women gracing the country's tourist brochures. The only things missing to complete the picture were the curly-tipped white cap, peplum, and plain wooden shoes. Instead, she wore a short-sleeved white blouse and a narrow gray pencil skirt that stopped an inch shy of her knees.

She was stunning. Harry could think of no better word.

"Harry." John greeted him with genuine warmth as he came from behind the desk to take Harry's proffered hand in both of his. "I want you to meet Marlies Wiersma, the intelligence officer I've assigned to your case." He stepped aside to include her in the conversation. "Marlies, this is Harry Jordan."

Her self-assured, dazzling smile revealed equally dazzling teeth. She shook his hand, her grip as firm as any man's. She seemed to be memorizing his face, no doubt well aware that she left him tongue-tied. Restless energy oozed from her pores. John's assistant had made him feel old and unimpressive, but this woman had him wrestling the inner dull fuddy-duddy Alcine, his Italian ex-girlfriend, had accused him of being.

"It's a pleasure to meet you, Mr. Jordan," Marlies said. "Call me Lies." She pronounced it *Lees*, with a soft *s* on the end.

He released her hand and regained his power of speech. "Harry."

John picked up a stack of papers and tucked them under his arm. "I have another meeting about to start. Harry, Lies is available as of today. I'll have Penny book her on the same flight as yours back to Amsterdam tonight, only she'll be flying economy, not business. These are taxpayer dollars I'm spending. Feel free to use my office while you two work out the logistics. I'll be back in an hour."

John left. Harry claimed the visitor chair next to Lies's and shifted it sideways so they were facing each other. She crossed those long legs, an action that slid her plain, narrow gray skirt up her thighs.

He cleared his throat and tried not to stare. He'd conduct this exchange as if it were a job interview, which in a way it was. "Have you ever worked as a personal assistant before?"

She hooked a short blond ringlet behind one ear, revealing a row of piercings with tiny diamond studs in them that winked in the sunlight.

"I've worked at a lot of things," she assured him. "Don't worry. I'll do my homework. That's what the Internet is for. I also trust you'll point out anything I do that might draw unwanted attention."

She was going to draw attention by breathing. John had to be out of his mind to think a young woman such as Marlies Wiersma, simply because she could speak the language, would be the right intelligence officer to handle someone like Bernard Vanderloord.

In his late forties, Vanderloord was what could best be described as a player when it came to the opposite sex. Alcine had fallen for him and she should have known better. Lies, while strikingly beautiful, gave off the air of a varsity athlete, not a sophisticated femme fatale. Vanderloord, a shark, would take one look at her and spot easy prey.

And then Harry realized how much of a dull fuddy-duddy he really was, because no doubt that was John's objective. Lies—young, pretty, and ambitious—was bait.

Did Harry approve?

Not in the least. It left a bad taste in his mouth. But it wasn't his call. All he had to do was satisfy himself that she could pull off her role as his personal assistant. The rest was John's problem.

He fired a barrage of questions at her, most of which she answered either to his satisfaction or with skillful evasion, and he was impressed. She was smart. He made note of the areas where she'd need to be coached.

Then, it was her turn to grill him.

"Can you tell me a little about how the trade commission functions?" she asked. "Who works in your defense department? How many people come through in the run of a day? What is your client base?"

As far as his entire client base was concerned, he wasn't going there. The only one who concerned her was Vanderloord. The rest didn't need CSIS nosing around in their business.

"One of our clients is the reason I'm here." He'd already told John his story, and John had no doubt filled her in, at least in part, but Harry would repeat it to make sure Lies understood what she was getting into. "Bernard Vanderloord is a Canadian ex-pat who does business all over the world, primarily with military contracts. Basically, he acts as a third-party broker, buying and selling manufactured parts for maintenance and repair. I have reason to believe that some of those aircraft parts in particular are being purchased for one purpose, then modified, re-categorized, and sold for a secondary purpose. Europe's open borders are convenient for moving re-purposed goods from one country, then shipped from a second or third country to circumvent trade embargos. It works a lot like money laundering."

John had said Lies was an expert on that subject, and she was nodding, so Harry continued. "The euro is fast becoming the currency of choice for money laundering, surpassing the American dollar, because of the number of countries that use it and because it can move across borders without being traced. So, not only has Vanderloord been trafficking in military goods, but he's also exchanging currency. He's set up a sort of hawala system in at least ten different countries, including Canada. You know what that is?"

She nodded again. "Yes. It's an informal value transfer system. Money is given to a broker in one country, who calls a broker in a second country to release that amount to the intended recipient, minus a percentage. The brokers either exchange equal value goods or services for the cash, or hold a credit against a future cash exchange. Since a hawala system operates on a high level of trust, I'm assuming Mr. Vanderloord is using companies he's either invested in or has a working relationship with."

"For the most part." He was trying to establish working relationships with Harry's connections to further his networks and Harry wasn't having it.

"How did you find out all of this?"

The tips of his ears began to burn. "The wife of an Albanian diplomat. She took me aside at an art event at their embassy in The Hague to tell me."

Lies dissected that piece of information and came to the same conclusion he had. "She was sleeping with Vanderloord and he ended the relationship."

"That would be a reasonable assumption, yes." His face had to be matching his ears by now. The Albanian diplomat should have known better than to marry his mistress. *If she'll do it with you, she'll do it to you*, to paraphrase Dr. Phil. "It also means her information is suspect. She could be trying to get even with him. To be honest, she's dramatic and politics isn't her strong suit. She might have misunderstood something she overheard and blown it out of proportion."

But he didn't believe that, and he could tell by the slight inward, thoughtful drawing of Lies's pretty red lips that she knew he didn't.

He shifted the conversation off his clients and onto the daily operations of his office. Lies had a number of language skills besides Dutch that might come in handy, although when it came to sharing the details of her educational background, she was understandably vague.

After that, the conversation started to drag. A surreptitious glance at his watch warned Harry that John was overdue from his meeting. Harry couldn't simply walk out of the office. He worked with the military and this wasn't his first trip to National Headquarters in Ottawa so he knew the drill. Someone had to escort him downstairs to security so he could sign out and turn in his visitor pass.

Besides, he had a few things to discuss with John in private. The diplomat's angry, sobbing, mistress-turned-wife left him unconvinced that a female intelligence officer handling Vanderloord was the best approach to be taking. Things could get messy and ugly, and he didn't want an international incident unfolding on Dutch soil. Their shipbuilding industry had strong connections to Canada. Not to mention, this whole setup made him feel like a pimp.

And he hadn't given John the whole story either. He'd left Alcine out of it. She swore she'd told Vanderloord nothing about the trade commission's business and Harry believed her.

There'd be very little for her to tell anyway. He'd never indulged in pillow talk.

"If you have work to do, I don't mind waiting for John alone," he hinted to Lies.

"I can't leave you alone, especially in the director's private office."

"Of course not. I wasn't thinking." Now he felt like an idiot. But he was struggling to find a casual topic of conversation with a beautiful woman in a context that was outside his usual frame of reference. If this were a social setting, he'd have no problem. At work, also not an issue. This wasn't either of those. "I take it you're familiar with the Netherlands already. What's your favorite place?"

She flashed him that dazzling smile. It warned him she knew how uncomfortable he was and she'd use it as leverage if he gave her half a chance.

"The whole country is beautiful," she said. "I do have to say, though, I have a particular attachment to Friesland. I have family there."

They'd found common ground. He relaxed, although he didn't let down his guard. "One of our biggest shipbuilding clients has offices in Friesland. I've taken a tour. For my own personal preference though, I like Leiden." He shrugged. "There's something about the youth and the enthusiasm of an international university town I find fascinating."

"Because you forget what it's like to be young?" She lifted one dark blond eyebrow and rubbed the tips of her long fingers along the tubular steel arm of her chair, a sparkle in her eyes making their blue depths appear even more vivid. "You aren't such an old man."

Her gentle teasing came from nowhere, changing the pattern his thoughts had been making from a straight line to a tangled maze he couldn't maneuver. In any other situation he'd almost think she was flirting with him, but she wasn't a social acquaintance, employee, or friend. Because he didn't know how to classify her, he wasn't quite sure where to take the conversation from here. Since she was CSIS, however, he'd sure as hell never be able to trust her enough to let down his guard. Their interactions, if he couldn't convince John to replace her, were going to fall somewhere between informal and official. That translated to awkward and she'd take full advantage of it, as she was trying to do now.

She was a spy. He'd do best to remember it. Whatever game she was planning to play, he'd sit on the sidelines and mind his own business. Unfortunately, he couldn't warn anyone else in his office or circle of acquaintances that she'd come in contact with. He hoped there wouldn't be too much collateral damage.

"Not so much old," he conceded dryly, "as wise. I do have a few years of experience behind me."

Before she could comment on that, John reappeared. He strode into the room and tossed his papers on the desk. "How'd we make out?" he asked, his manner suggesting he believed the planning he'd left them to do had gone off without any hitches.

Not true.

"I'd like a few words with you," Harry said to him.

Lies knew when she was being dismissed. She gathered the file John had given her earlier, shuffling the loose pages inside it so they were lined up neat and tidy with the edges, then stood.

"I'll read this before I leave the office," she said to her director, holding the file up in one hand. "I'm going to head home this afternoon to pack."

She might not need to do so after Harry had John alone. She'd definitely picked up on a vibe that said he didn't want her working with him. She suspected he was going to try and talk John into handing this assignment to another intelligence officer, most likely a man. In retaliation, she'd had to poke him a little by teasing him about his sober personality.

Get with the times, Mr. Jordan. Women work in espionage too. In fact, they've done so for centuries.

He stood with her, all gentlemanly politeness. At five foot ten, or maybe an inch more, he was around the same height as she. He wasn't heavy or thin, handsome or homely. He had nice brown eyes with lashes almost as long as a girl's, tipping the man-meter scales to attractive. He wore his brown hair military-cut short. So far, there were no touches of gray or hints of male pattern baldness. His suit and shoes screamed understated but expensive, and fit him very well. It was obvious he kept in good physical condition. Lies decided that, even though vanity was the more powerful motivator for most people, Harry worked out to fend off stress. He wasn't the most Zen person she'd ever met.

And yet he didn't give the impression of a man who made many mistakes. He also knew how to keep his cards close to his chest, evading any questions she'd posed that he'd deemed too personal when it came to either him, his staff, or his business associates. She itched to find out what he was hiding. His personal secrets wouldn't be deep and dark—he practically glowed with integrity—but she suspected they might prove interesting, because Harry had something deeper going for him. He was charismatic in a quiet way that had encouraged a woman who'd been jilted by a lover to entrust him with a secret that could cost her life. Arms dealing and money laundering—for that was what Vanderloord was doing—weren't things nice people did, no matter how they tried to dress it up. Lies had personal experience.

The pain of loss and humiliation, still fresh, squeezed her heart. She wasn't ready to take on another assignment where she was expected to get close to a man. That was the real reason she'd helped sabotage herself by poking fun at Harry. He'd be presenting his case against her the second she walked out the door and a part of her hoped for his success. Mind games were one thing. Games of the heart quite another, and hers was still fragile.

He extended his hand. "It was a pleasure meeting you, Lies."

He had a nice grip—longer than indifference, but not so long as to become off-putting to women. He didn't say he'd see her at the airport, or in The Hague, or that he looked forward to working with her, confirming her suspicions that he planned to have her replaced. She murmured something equally polite, nodded to John who was watching their interaction and not missing a nuance, and slipped out of the office, closing the door behind her with a soft snick.

A clock on the cream-colored wall of the outer office shouted that it was already almost time for a coffee break, and so far this morning, she hadn't even made it as far as her desk.

She spoke a few words to John's assistant Penny as she passed her desk, then, out in the common area of the department, worked her way through the maze of cubicles to her own. She dropped the file in her top desk drawer, grabbed her empty coffee cup, and went to fill it in the break room before returning to her workspace for a few hours of light reading.

Before she was completely resettled, a tiny paper Canadian flag mounted on a wooden stick popped up over one wall of her cubicle, followed by a head.

Dan, her team leader. He came around the partition and made himself at home in the tiny plastic visitor's chair.

"Truce?" he asked.

"That depends on if you brought chocolate."

He passed her a small white bag from a nearby specialty store. "I wouldn't do this kissing up for just anyone, you know."

Of course not. Most of his team members were men smart enough not to sleep with their targets. Granted, that was because most of their targets were also men. Plus, Dan had sold her out. She hadn't forgotten that part, no matter how good he believed his reason for it to be. There was a double standard at play here.

That didn't mean she wasn't taking his chocolate. At the end of the day, double standard or not, Lies was the one who'd made the mistake. How Dan chose to address it was his prerogative. She loved her job and she wanted to keep it.

"Thank you," she said, opening the bag and peeking inside. "I'm not sharing it with you."

"I know you think I treated you differently, and maybe I did," Dan began, diving right in. "But there's a lot at stake on this assignment. I don't want anyone's overpaid lawyer calling your integrity into question."

So Dan knew about the defense minister's involvement, even if she wouldn't be reporting to him.

Did she really want to take on the Minister of National Defence?

She popped a milk chocolate, hazelnut praline into her

mouth, mulling his words over. No one's lawyer would have any reason to come gunning for her. She gathered information which CSIS then passed on to the appropriate authorities. It wasn't up to CSIS, a civilian organization, to prove the value of her information in court. That was a problem for law enforcement officers.

And the Minister of National Defence wasn't above the law.

A rush of adrenaline swept through her. She could do this.

"Your kissing up is accepted," she mumbled around a mouthful of sweet, gooey goodness, hoping Harry lost his argument with John after all.

CHAPTER TWO

THE AIRPORT LOUNGE WAS quiet this evening.

Harry, seated alone at the bar, stared into his beer. He'd bumped Lies's ticket to business class so she'd be seated with him for the journey—since for all intents and purposes she was now his PA—and then left a message for her to meet him here. They had to make a short domestic hop to Toronto to meet their connecting flight to Amsterdam and a quick check of his watch said she was cutting it close. He'd hoped to establish certain boundaries before they reached Amsterdam and had to put on a show. The confined cabin of an aircraft wasn't the place for that discussion.

John had refused to reconsider assigning her to his office. "She's the best person for you, Harry. Trust me. She'll get the job done. You're telling me he has a weakness for young, beautiful women. He's also been trying to work his way into your office. Lies will get him a foot in the door without you having to do an about-face that might make him suspicious."

That last was true enough. Something about Vanderloord had rubbed Harry the wrong way from the first, and the incident with Alcine had sealed his opinion.

He made it a personal policy to avoid doing business with anyone he didn't believe he could trust and he'd turned down several meeting requests from Vanderloord already. Lies, new to the staff and inexperienced, could accept the next one on his behalf.

She slid onto the stool beside him.

She wore a pair of tight-fitting tan leggings and a lightweight white blazer. Her shoes were beige canvas flats and matched the bag she was carrying. Her short mass of blond ringlets had been drawn back from her face and tamed by a white hairband. She looked exactly like a fresh-faced young professional on a business trip, casual but not careless about her appearance, so he couldn't say why he had this sense of impending disaster. He had no basis for his belief she'd never be able to pull this off. He knew nothing about her other than that she was a spy.

Maybe he really was all doom and gloom—another one of Alcine's complaints about him when they'd ended their relationship.

Lies's knee kissed his thigh as she got comfortable on the stool. All his nerve endings cried danger. He shifted his leg away, trying not to be obvious, uncertain as to whether the intimate contact was deliberate or not. She was a flirt who enjoyed playing games and he found her far too attractive to best her at this one.

"Sorry I'm late," she said. "I had extra bags to check and it was a bit of a production. Airlines are ruthless."

Of course she'd have a lot of luggage. He should have arranged for them to arrive at the airport together so he could help her with it. He carried an overnight bag because he was only in Canada for a few days, but she'd had to pack for an indeterminate stay in The Hague.

He drained the last of his beer and signaled the

bartender for another. "Can I buy you a drink?"

"I'll have a cola."

The bartender brought them their drinks and Harry paid his tab. He picked up his glass, looked around the empty room, then reached for the overnight bag and laptop on the floor at his feet. "Let's move to a table where we can talk."

He tucked his belongings under the table out of their way and held Lies's chair for her before seating himself.

"I wanted to go over a few of your duties with you," he began.

"I'll be an awesome personal assistant, Harry," she assured him with a level of confidence he had to admire. "You won't regret hiring me. Nobody expects someone new to a position to hit the ground running, and I'm not afraid to ask questions."

That was a large part of the problem. He didn't want her interrogating his staff and associates. He knew exactly how much intelligence someone could gather by feigning ignorance. She was a wolf in sheep's clothing and he was turning her loose on an unsuspecting flock. So when he said duties, he really meant boundaries.

He'd already figured out she'd have little respect for his authority. John Carmichael was her real boss, not him.

"I'm not worried about day to day operations." He took a swig of his beer. He didn't plan to give her free access to embassy files. CSIS didn't need to have its nose in all his affairs. "A big part of my job involves social functions and dinners, and you should accompany me. It's the easiest way for you to get to know the right people. You won't have much free time in the evenings."

"In my last position I was on call pretty much twenty-four seven. I'm used to long hours." She looked at the drink in her hand. It trembled a little and she set it down with too much precision. Harry wondered what that was about. Maybe she wasn't as confident with this assignment as she'd have him believe. She ran one finger up and down the sweating glass. Her eyebrows rose, drawing his gaze to her eyes, and once again he was caught up in how blue they were. "Who would you normally take to dinner?"

Again he had to wonder if she was flirting with him, and if so, what her purpose for it might be. If it was to unsettle him, mission accomplished.

He had an urge, no doubt bolstered by the beer, to shake all that feminine confidence. "My girlfriend recently ended our relationship. No one will think it odd for me to bring my young, very attractive, new personal assistant with me."

Lies's expression changed. Compassion filtered into her eyes and she leaned toward him, ever so slightly, before drawing back as if changing her mind about whatever she'd been about to say or do. "I'm sorry."

"Don't be. It was overdue." Alcine had always been more interested in the lifestyle than him. Her interest in Vanderloord, however, had been the final straw. He pushed his unfinished beer away. He'd had enough to drink, especially since he had to watch what he said around Lies.

She was studying him. A slight frown tugged at her finely-arched brows. He knew what she saw—a dull, middle-aged businessman of passing good looks. The most exciting thing about him was his career and that could hardly impress a CSIS intelligence officer. She leaned on her forearms, bringing her head closer to his from across the small table.

"In order to do my job, I need to know where I fit in your life," Lies said. "Am I someone you overlook because you see me as unimportant, or do I have a position of power with you? Do you confide in me or do I carry your bags? Do I know every detail of your life, both personal and professional, or do I know nothing about you at all beyond your work schedule?"

He hadn't thought that far ahead and didn't like to make quick decisions. "Does it matter? Do we need to know that right now?"

"It does and we do." She placed her hand over his, adding another layer of intimacy to the discussion, as if they were well acquainted already. She leaned closer still until their noses were scant inches apart. "Crime bosses go for the top of the food chain or the bottom. The middle's not worth their time." She stroked the tip of one finger across the back of his wrist. Whether the gesture was absent-minded or calculated, he couldn't tell. He did know it was distracting. "Why do you suppose the ambassador's wife was a target? And she was, Harry. He got more than a good time from her. She probably knows it too, but is afraid to admit it. That makes me very curious about the information she gave you. If it's accurate, why did he underestimate her so badly? Is it possible she told you things he meant for you to hear?"

She posed very good questions.

"Dita isn't exactly what one would describe as sophisticated," Harry explained carefully. "She's a former model and quite attractive. She's also only twenty-three years old compared to her husband's sixty-seven. It's possible she wasn't the target in this case, but doing some targeting herself, and got more than she expected."

A smile of enlightenment curled Lies's pink-tinted lips. "So you're suggesting she's working her way out of Albania… Let me guess. The story she gave you came with a plea for protection and an offer you couldn't resist." Her smile brightened, a hint of laughter lurking in her eyes. "Although I'd bet money you did."

He wasn't stupid. Or a naïve twenty-three year old. And yet Lies made him feel as if he were both. A flush of heat that had nothing to do with a tight tie or the beer he'd consumed crept up his neck. "I'm not interested in women who play games—especially dangerous ones."

Let her make of that what she would.

If anything, it amused her even more. "We still haven't settled the question of whether I'm a low-level staff member you have little time for, and basically ignore, or someone you keep close to you."

"Close," he said far too quickly, but there was no way he could afford to ignore her and he didn't care if she knew it. Someone had to protect the innocent and unsuspecting. He flipped his hand over so their palms connected and he laced their fingers together, ignoring an image in his head of how far they could take this charade. Then he laid out what he believed to be the best scenario under the circumstances. "I'd like to be sleeping with you, but you want to keep things professional between us to protect your career. You're ambitious, but you know better than to sleep with your boss."

Her fingers stiffened in his. A muscle puckered one corner of her mouth as she straightened and withdrew her hand.

"That's our flight, Mr. Jordan," she said.

"Pardon?"

At first he thought he must have struck a nerve, which was why she was suddenly so formal, and puzzled over what he'd said wrong. Maybe she'd misinterpreted his words, taking them too literally, and was offended.

Maybe she'd read his mind.

The collar on his shirt shrank a size over that last possibility.

"The announcement?" She waved a finger at the ceiling, indicating the airport's public address system. "They're calling our flight."

There was nothing wrong with her nerves or his words, then. His collar loosened its grip. She'd simply slipped into the role he'd assigned her, and with an ease that left his head spinning.

He slung the strap of his laptop over one shoulder, then picked up his black leather overnight bag and squeezed the rubber grip on the handle. He would never have hired a woman like Marlies Wiersma as a personal assistant and she was going to cause speculation among the people who knew him.

But as far as spies went, he acknowledged John really might well know what he was doing. Lies was a chameleon. It would be interesting to watch how she chose to play Vanderloord. He hitched the laptop strap higher.

What wasn't so interesting was how easily she could play him.

They landed at Schiphol close to noon local time. Harry had a car waiting for them, a luxury Lies was unused to.

She asked to be dropped off at an address on the outskirts of The Hague she'd been given. CSIS kept flats in major cities across Europe for intelligence use. This one was in an area of the city housing a number of immigrants and students, and perhaps not so coincidentally, Canadian ex-pats. Vanderloord would never live in a low-end neighborhood such as this, but here, she could keep her eyes and ears open as to what activities others living abroad might be involved in.

Harry made a face when he saw the building, but said nothing. Lies shrugged off his unspoken disapproval. Not everyone who worked for the government could live in the luxury flats surrounding the Canadian embassy in the heart of the city.

He insisted on walking up with her so he could help carry her bags despite her assurances that she could manage. The flat wouldn't meet his high standards, but that was his problem, not hers.

The elevator was out of commission. The stairs off the main entry of the building were narrow and steep, and smelled funky, like urine. Her flat was on the third floor, accessible from an outdoor walkway encircling the building. By the time she unlocked the door and they'd dragged all her luggage inside, he was frowning.

It wasn't fancy, even she had to admit. But it wasn't awful either. It was tiny, with a combined living room and kitchenette, and through an open door, she caught sight of a shower in a corner of the bedroom. The entrance had a small toilet enclosure and enough room for her to store a bicycle, which was the best way to travel and what everyone used. The train station was nearby so she'd have no problem getting to and from work. They'd passed a schoolyard down the street too, meaning the neighborhood would be reasonably safe. Parents tended to be vigilant.

And it was furnished.

"Isn't this cozy!" she exclaimed, just to see how Harry would react.

He gazed around the entire flat from the safety of the half-open doorway. "I'll find you accommodations closer to the embassy."

It would be a mistake. Lies might be Canadian, born and raised in that country, but she'd been taught traditional Dutch values. Her family wasn't rich but they had money, and the thought of flaunting it would appall them. She couldn't work with the Dutch staff at the Canadian embassy and live in a flat no one else could afford. She'd never earn their trust or respect. If this was going to work, she had to be just what she seemed at all times.

"No thank you," she said.

Harry's jaw set in a hard, stubborn line. "I told you, you'll have to work late hours. You can't walk this neighborhood late at night by yourself."

She could be stubborn too. She was here on assignment as an intelligence officer. He didn't have any real authority to dictate how she was to live or behave while she was here, or interfere in her case simply because she was a woman, and she couldn't afford to allow him to. John and Dan had both intimated that CSIS had a lot riding on this case. She'd been given a second chance not to screw up and she planned to prove just how good she could be at her job.

Her job didn't have to be boring however.

She widened her eyes. "That's right. I forgot that you're supposed to be pursuing me. Granted I've only known you a short while so I could be mistaken, but it seems out of character for you to be setting an employee up as your mistress. Picking an embassy apartment for me might be crossing a line. I'll be fine here."

His too serious, too honest brown eyes warned her he wasn't used to anyone challenging his decisions, or making jokes at his expense—which meant she found it fascinating to do so. Her heart revved up in spontaneous anticipation. He'd been standoffish from the moment she'd met him, posing a challenge she couldn't seem to resist. She wondered what his breaking point was.

And then he reached for the handle on the door, preparing to leave without a fight, ruining her fun. "I'll send a car for you tomorrow morning."

"I'm already familiar with the transit system here," she reminded him, pushing a little bit harder. "The Netherlands is a second home to me. I can get to the Canadian embassy on my own."

"Very well. If you're sure."

Then he was gone and she was staring at the peeling paint on the closed door, disappointed Harry had opted not to react.

Goading him was harmless fun. He was safe, predictable, and no way did he live life on the edge. He was as unlike Michael as it was possible for two men to be. But that didn't mean he wasn't complicated.

Perhaps that was why she couldn't leave him alone.

She discovered clean linen in a cupboard and made up the bed. They'd traveled all night and she was exhausted, but she didn't want to sleep the whole afternoon away, preferring to adjust to the six-hour time difference as fast as she could. Without unpacking or doing more than wash her face, she set the alarm for two hours and crawled between the welcoming sheets.

Later that day, she went out to the shops and picked up a few groceries to have on hand for the morning—a loaf of bread, a brick of cheese, and a selection of fruits and juices. Her flat had a coffee maker so she bought a package of coffee too. She found a café and sipped a fresh-brewed cup at an outdoor table while she sat in the warm sun and observed the activity on the street.

The neighborhood wasn't as bad as Harry believed. Eclectic, yes. But Lies, used to life in Ottawa and the ethnic diversity of Canadian cities, barely noticed that. Political tensions ran higher here than at home, and people tended to segregate more, so the mixture of cultures in the community was nice to see. And Dutch streets were so neat and tidy. She loved that. Tomorrow, or before the end of the week, she'd have to buy herself a bicycle so she could explore.

In her head she ran over the case file she'd read on Bernard Vanderloord. It contained surprisingly little for someone involved in all his purported activities, but enough that his cross-border dealings should have appeared on Interpol's radar long before this. The usual procedure was for them to alert the Royal Canadian Mounted Police, who in turn, would notify CSIS to investigate. So why hadn't that happened?

A few of the pages in the report had been redacted, another curious thing. There had been a grainy digital photo, an address for his main residence, and a brief history of his life in Canada before he left the country. Forty-seven years of age, he'd grown up in Quebec and attended McGill University, one of the finest educational facilities in the country. As far as anyone knew, he'd never been married. He threw lavish, under-the-radar private New Year parties and invited the entire diplomatic community as guests in an unofficial capacity, as well as senior representatives of the Dutch government. Harry probably attended too, despite having rebuffed any attempts Vanderloord made to do business with Canada's Department of National Defence or its contractors. It would be a networking opportunity too good for either of them to pass up.

Normally anyone involved in activities like money laundering and espionage would give Harry, who wore his integrity like a badge of honor, a wide berth. He'd be incorruptible and not worth the effort, so the continued overtures on Vanderloord's part to get to know him made Lies very curious. That would be the first thing she looked into. What was it about Harry that Vanderloord couldn't seem to resist?

And why, if Vanderloord had a connection to the defense minister, did he not try and leverage that friendship instead? Why pursue Harry openly, but keep the ministerial connection so secret?

Wednesday morning, Lies joined the crowd on the train headed into the heart of the city. From the Mauritskade stop in The Hague's city center, she made her way to the Canadian embassy.

At the embassy she had to pass through a security check. Harry had already cleared her by arranging for a temporary ID. One of the trade commission assistants, an attractive woman in her early fifties, came to the main entrance to escort her through the building. Her name was Hannah Leary, and she had a wide, pleasant smile that poorly concealed her curiosity. If her reaction was anything to judge by, Harry bringing in a new staff member unannounced was already creating a stir.

The Defence trade commission offices were on the second floor. Hannah showed Lies where the washrooms were located and then ushered her to a small, empty office. "Harry's office is next door. He's tied up on the phone at the moment. He'll come get you when he's free."

So Lies was going to be cut off from the rest of the trade commission staff. It was the sort of thing she'd expect someone like Harry, who couldn't quite hide his distrust of her or her profession, to do. He wouldn't want his coworkers on CSIS's radar.

He needn't worry. The only embassy employee on her radar was Harry.

Almost an hour later, when she was ready to pass out from boredom, Harry appeared at the door.

"Sorry about that," he said. "I had an important phone call that couldn't wait. Why don't you come into my office so we can go over your duties?"

Since he'd approached CSIS, not the other way around, Lies would have thought she'd be near the top of his priorities too, but held her peace.

He ushered her into his office and shut the door. He smiled, turning his normal serious expression into one that made him appear years younger, and really, quite sexy. "I've told staff that you're here on a temporary placement while awaiting a permanent assignment. They might have gotten the impression your father is important in diplomatic circles. It will explain why you attend so many evening functions with me. They'll think I'm keeping an eye on you for him."

A good night's sleep and implementing a plan he'd thought through without any input from her had apparently done wonders for Harry's sense of control. He reeked of relief and she couldn't have that.

"I'm disappointed," she said. "I was really looking forward to being seduced by you."

His expression never altered. "In retrospect, that plan would never have worked."

"Why not?" she asked, genuinely curious and oddly let down as to why he'd abandoned Plan A. "It was simple enough, and you've got to admit, the track record for that particular ploy is pretty successful."

"No one would believe it. I'm hardly your type. You aren't mine either."

He was being practical, not trying to insult her, and while he was right on both counts, she debated the benefits of pointing out that stranger things had happened. As long as Vanderloord bought in, what did it matter what Harry's staff thought?

"You don't know what my type is. Maybe I like uptight trade commissioners."

"You like corrupting them. I don't like being corrupted." That disarming smile reappeared, adding warmth to his eyes and taking the sting out of his words.

He was right yet again. His comfort zone was so much smaller than hers. She liked men who were willing to take risks and anyone could see Harry was a looker, not a leaper. They were a definite mismatch.

Maybe Vanderloord pursued him because he enjoyed the challenge Harry presented. She'd already figured out the entertainment factor in that too, and could appreciate the attraction.

"At least being the spoiled daughter of an important diplomat gives me freedom." She sighed. "I bet I'm a hell-raiser."

Again, warmth slid into his eyes. "I bet you are too. I pity your father."

She couldn't help smiling back. "He'll survive. He's had plenty of time to get used to me. What's more important—does Bernard Vanderloord prefer hell-raising women?"

She watched Harry mull that question over with typical care.

"He likes arm candy," he finally said. "He prefers them young, fun, beautiful, and not especially bright. You've got three out of four qualities more or less covered. I'm not sure he'd equate hell-raising with fun so you might want to tone that one down."

He made teasing him way too easy. "If I've got three out of four qualities covered, are you suggesting I'm not especially bright?"

His good humor faded. "Exactly the opposite, Ms. Wiersma. Unfortunately, Vanderloord is bright too. Something for you to remember."

"They always are." The mistake people like Vanderloord made was in forgetting that other people weren't necessarily stupid. Arrogance was their downfall. It had also been hers and she'd learned the pitfalls of discounting another person's intelligence the hard way. "But I'll keep it in mind." She'd baited Harry enough for one morning. It was time to get down to work. "Right now I need a list of your clients, current and over the past two years."

"I'll see what I can do." He reached for a folder on his desk. "While you're waiting, you can reconcile my credit card statements and business expenses. I've asked Hannah to set you up with a computer. She's already put in an order."

Lies took the file from him and flipped through it. "Business expenses, hmm? You're giving me access to a lot of information."

"If you find anything exciting I'll take you to dinner. On second thought," he said before she could come up with a clever response, "I'll take you to dinner anyway. Then I'll drive you home. This afternoon I'll look into renting one of the embassy's flats for you."

She was annoyed and impressed in equal measure. He was determined to have his own way, which came as no real surprise, but he was more devious than she'd credited him for. His change in cover story made more sense to her now. The spoiled daughter of a diplomat would expect better housing.

Annoyance won out. "I already have plans for dinner," she lied. "I don't need a drive and I'm OK with the flat I have now. The neighborhood is perfectly safe, Harry. So is the public transit system."

He folded his arms across his chest and held her gaze. "Think of what your father would say if he knew where you were living."

She lifted her chin, refusing to be the first to look away. "He'd say I'm twenty-eight years old and a trained intelligence officer who can look after herself."

"You're twenty-eight?" Harry sounded genuinely surprised.

"How old did you think I was?"

"I don't know," he admitted. "Young. Younger than that, I mean."

His assessment of her was based solely on emotion, not fact. She looked her age, or at least most people thought so, which meant he found her immature—and all because she'd disagreed with him over a few things that weren't any of his business.

OK, maybe he did have a few facts on his side. She'd been doing her best to get a rise out of him since the moment they met, which didn't speak to a high level of emotional maturity.

"I'd like to believe I'm not quite ready for a nursing home," she replied. "When I am though, maybe you can put in a good word for me at yours. You seem to have settled in nicely."

His left eye developed a tic. He turned the conversation back to the original topic. "Don't make too many more dinner plans," he advised her. "Your real work will start after hours. And most of it will take place around the embassy here in the city's center, so I'm not sure why you want to make it more difficult."

Because that wasn't why he was offering her embassy accommodations, and if she were a male officer, it would never occur to him to make such a proposition.

She was going to give in. She spared a small pang of regret for the neighborhood she wasn't going to get to explore. This wasn't a battle worth fighting and he wasn't necessarily wrong. She hated, however, to lose, and her irritation was real. Taking an embassy flat was going to have an impact on her ability to interact with the other staff in his office. She couldn't be a spoiled rich girl with Vanderloord and a simple office worker with them.

"I'll take the flat. But in the future," she said, "I prefer to make my own decisions. Moving will limit my abilities to gather information from other sources."

"You're here to gather it from Vanderloord." He gestured toward the folder in her hand. "And while you're here in the office, you have to keep up appearances. Do you need Hannah to show you how to reconcile those?"

She finally got it. His real objective wasn't her safety. It was to limit her ability to communicate with his staff on an equal footing. Her annoyance flipped over to admiration. He knew the culture. He wasn't the only one who'd missed a few facts when making an assessment.

She'd been well played.

CHAPTER THREE

LIES STEPPED BACK AND surveyed the results of her handiwork. This had to be the ugliest wall she'd ever seen.

It was a late Saturday afternoon. She'd been in the Netherlands for a little better than two weeks and she was spending the weekend with her cousin Yasmin in Haarlem, helping to paint her new house.

Bernard Vanderloord had been out of the country since before her arrival and keeping up with Harry's paperwork while she waited for his return was dull as dirt. She'd wanted to do something that would get her mind off her lack of progress at work, so here she was.

Yasmin had seen a color scheme in a magazine she'd admired and wanted to try it in her living room. She'd sectioned off one wall with tape into hundreds of squares, then cut the squares into diamonds. Each individual diamond was painted one of five different shades of five different colors, creating a bold, kaleidoscopic effect.

It was only paint, nothing that couldn't be covered when impetuous Yasmin grew bored with it a few months from now, as history suggested she would. Lies, however, couldn't imagine a look more inappropriate for a beautiful old townhouse that was showing its age. The cupboards sagged in the adjoining kitchen. The tracks for the sliding glass doors that led from the dining area past the narrow kitchen to the overgrown garden beyond had begun to rot to the point Lies was concerned about security. Yasmin should worry more about break-ins, and fix that problem first, rather than spend a small fortune on paint for one wall.

The garden was solidly fenced in however, and bordered on either side as it was by its neighbors, relatively inaccessible to passersby. The lock on the gate leading to the street behind the row houses was sturdy. Anyone trying to get in would have to be very athletic and determined, so maybe spending the money on paint wasn't such a big deal and Lies should learn to let Yasmin look out for herself.

If she were in her cousin's shoes, she wouldn't listen to unsolicited advice either. Fearlessness was a family curse.

"I love it," Yasmin declared.

The fine paintbrush she held dripped lemon yellow onto the drop cloth protecting warped hardwood floors that badly needed a new finish. Even though she was three years younger than Lies and sported short, spiky dark hair tipped in purple rather than blond curls, and deep, midnight blue eyes instead of cornflower, the two women were often mistaken for sisters. They were close enough that they felt as if they were.

Lies bit her tongue and began wrapping her own brush in plastic to save it to use again the next day. This was Yasmin's first home and she'd fallen deeply in love with it. The questionable paint job and overall dilapidation aside, Lies could appreciate its appeal. The neighborhood primarily housed young couples starting their families and the elderly who'd either lived here their entire adult lives or were downsizing. These were the perfect starter homes for young professionals, particularly women living alone, and she liked it a lot more than the neighborhood around the embassy flat that Harry had forced on her. Here, children played in the street and people greeted each other by name. The Hague's city center was overrun by tourists and people like Harry who used it for business and entertaining.

After two weeks of dinner meetings and formal evening receptions, she could safely say that, as absorbing as it was to try and peer beneath people's public façades, she had no desire to lead such a lifestyle herself. It was artificial and constraining, and it surprised her that Harry, who was so...*real*, never showed a hint of impatience.

Not even with her, and she'd done her best to get under his skin.

"Why don't we get cleaned up and go out for dinner?" Yasmin suggested, adding a few more strokes to the wall with an intense concentration out of proportion to the task. "I have a new friend I'd like you to meet. He owns a restaurant nearby. I've been seeing him for a few weeks."

The carelessness in her tone caught Lies's attention because it didn't match the level of detail in her announcement. Lies pressed the lid tight on the paint can she'd been using, tapping it with the plastic handle of her brush to seal it, and took her time before responding. At twenty-five, and with a good job as an office manager, Yasmin was capable of making independent decisions about men. If this new friend owned a restaurant, then he must have ambition and a decent work ethic.

So why did Yasmin sound as if she wanted a second opinion? What was wrong with this new friend?

Lies wiped her hands on a rag. It was possible Yasmin simply wasn't ready for her family to find out she was seeing someone who might have staying power. Yasmin's brother Pieter could be overprotective of his younger sister—and of Lies too, for that matter. She'd suffered from it during her annual summer visits, so if Yasmin was trying to hide a fledgling relationship from him, she wasn't unsympathetic.

But Pieter wasn't always wrong when he ran his interventions. Yasmin was an exceptionally pretty girl, and in a country where blonds were the norm, she stood out.

"I'd love to meet him," Lies said.

An hour later they were walking the short distance to the restaurant. The cracked mortar between the bricks in the sidewalk caught at Lies's skinny boot heels. The uneven cobblestones on the streets made for rough walking too. Both women wore tight jeans they'd tucked into tall boots and draped colorful scarves over the collars of filmy blouses—Lies's was white and Yasmin's a deep, midnight blue that matched the shade of her eyes.

Fortunately, the restaurant was only five minutes away. It occupied a new and modern building at the center of a large square. The square was surrounded by local businesses intended to appeal to the whole family—a flower shop, a candy store, a pool hall, and arcade. The coffee shop was closed for the night but the small pub next door had a steady trickle of teenage patrons. It was too early for an adult crowd that wouldn't be going out for drinks until eleven.

Yasmin's friend had picked a respectable location for his enterprise, a point in his favor, although the inside of the low-ceilinged restaurant appeared to be a work in progress. The counter near the door held a battered cash register. Behind it was a door that led to the kitchen, judging by the smells and the sounds. The tables weren't fancy, the kind one saw at weddings in community halls with folding legs and thin plywood tops, and covered with simple white cotton cloths. Each table had a centerpiece consisting of a single candle stuck in an old wine bottle and surrounded by pretty flowers. The plain wooden chairs had seen better days, but looked sturdy enough for their intended purpose. The walls had what Lies assumed was local artwork hanging on them—some with prices attached.

And yet it all worked. The atmosphere inside leached friendly warmth. Patrons who obviously knew each other well chatted back and forth between the tables in the half-empty room.

"Yasmin!" a voice boomed.

A man in an enormous white apron strode from the kitchen and skirted the counter. He was tall, even more than the average, and about thirty years of age. Lies's dad would call him a string bean, but when middle-age spread settled in, he'd turn into a bear. He had light brown hair—likely blond when he was a child—and wore it tied in a knot at the back of his head.

He caught Yasmin in his arms and swung her off her feet before planting a solid kiss on her mouth. When he set her down she was breathless and beaming.

She introduced them, her arm around his waist and his draped over her shoulders. "Baart, meet my cousin Marlies. Lies, this is Baart."

Lies's Dutch, while impeccable, was textbook, and some of the dialects from the border towns were difficult for native speakers to follow. Baart's rapid-fire speech, laden with heavy overtones of Flemish, nearly defeated her. Before she knew what was happening, she too was hauled into an enthusiastic embrace and soundly kissed on both cheeks, European style.

"Welcome, Marlies. Come. Have a seat."

The women chose a table near the front window for no reason other than that from it, Lies could watch the small square outside as well as the restaurant's patrons within. A few minutes later, a bottle of red wine and two glasses arrived—compliments of the house.

Lies's heart plunged with disappointment. She and Yasmin shared a similar poor taste in men, if not paint, because Baart wasn't what he pretended to be. A quick glance around the restaurant assured her of that. She hoped Yasmin wasn't too deeply attached.

Yasmin took a sip of her wine, then leaned across the table. "You've met my friend. Now tell me about yours. You've been very quiet about him. Is everything OK?"

What made her think Harry was a boyfriend? Lies scanned her memory. What had she said that might have given Yasmin that impression?

Then she realized Yasmin was referring to Michael, who Lies had foolishly mentioned in a phone conversation a few months ago—not by name, but as someone she'd taken an interest in.

"It didn't work out." It no longer hurt to admit it. At least not as much.

"I could ask if Baart has a friend for you."

Yasmin watched closely for her response and Lies knew she was sounding her out for her opinion on the new man in Yasmin's life, but they weren't going to have this conversation in here. "We'll see."

Lies only half listened to Yasmin's chatter as they ate their meal. She was more interested in finding out what was going on inside the restaurant than Yasmin's plans for her house.

When it was time for them to leave, Baart refused to accept Lies's money. "I can't expect pretty ladies to pay."

He kissed Yasmin good-bye and waved to them from the door.

Out in the square, once he'd gone back inside and the door was closed, Yasmin turned to Lies with wary hope in her eyes. "What did you think of him?"

That Yasmin's brother Pieter would definitely overreact if he met Baart.

And if Yasmin had known Lies was an intelligence officer she probably wouldn't have introduced her to him either, but no one in the family knew what Lies did for a living other than that she worked for the government. Yasmin really believed she was a personal assistant on a short-term contract with the Canadian embassy.

Lies decided to tear off the Band-Aid rather than tug on it gently. "I think your boyfriend is a criminal." She counted with her fingers as she recited her reasons. "We were the only women in the restaurant and the only people who didn't know anyone else. Only two people paid for their meals and they used cash. Baart opened the till once all evening and that was to take money out. Nothing went in. Customers wandered in and out of his kitchen as if they owned it. And I think you already knew all of this was peculiar and it's why you brought me to meet him. You wanted a second opinion."

"He did seem too good to be true," Yasmin admitted, her expression woeful but hardly heartbroken, Lies was relieved to see.

"They always are. He doesn't have a key to your house, does he? You won't have any trouble breaking things off with him?" Lies asked, suddenly anxious. Baart might very well be doing nothing more than cheating on his taxes, but to Lies, the whole picture reeked of organized crime. If someone had fronted him money to set up his restaurant, Yasmin didn't need to be involved.

While legally Lies had no business collecting information on non-Canadians outside of Canada, she would if she had to.

"No." Yasmin brushed off that concern. "We aren't exclusive. I have a school friend who is with the police. I'll introduce them and that will be enough to make Baart lose interest."

Lies hoped he'd be that easy to shed. Yasmin was smart, pretty, and a lot of fun.

Although, Lies was relieved to see, more astute than she'd given her credit for. Unless Yasmin had any trouble with him, she wouldn't interfere.

"We're going for drinks," she decided. "And I want to go dancing. Let's have some fun."

She hooked her arm through Yasmin's and dragged her toward the pub in the far corner of the square.

Harry relaxed on the sofa in his living room, a glass of wine in his hand. Across from him sat his friend Lars, who worked for the Dutch *Kernfysische dienst*, the Department of Nuclear Safety, Security and Safeguards.

Harry had spent the past two weeks watching everything he said around Lies, and trying to interpret everything she said to him, and he was exhausted. Let someone else deal with her for the weekend.

Lars, while not as pretty, offered a welcome respite.

"There's been another report of a businessman who's gone missing in Russia," Lars was saying. A lick of blond hair that not even a generous application of gel had tamed stuck up at his temple. He sat with one ankle resting on the opposite knee. His left arm was slung along the back of the low, overstuffed chair in which his lanky frame slouched. Beside him, on a glass-topped end table, was an untouched drink. He'd accepted it to be polite, but in the three years Harry had known him, he'd rarely finished one.

"He knew the risks." Harry hated to sound cold, but it was true. People regularly took black market goods across the border into Russia because the profits to be had were significant. However, it was equally common for the trucks carrying those goods to go missing, and their drivers never heard from again. The cost of doing cross-border business in a country unofficially run by organized crime was high. And well known.

"This one was different." Lars frowned down the length of his arm at his drink, nudging the glass with a finger, causing its contents to sway dangerously close to the rim. "It's rumored his truck wasn't carrying television sets."

Harry waited. A tight knot had a stranglehold on his chest. Whatever his preoccupied friend debated telling him, it was serious.

Lars dropped his foot to the floor and his arm to his knee. He leaned toward Harry, his face troubled. "You didn't learn this from me. A reliable source heard from a less reliable one that the missing truck contained refurbished aircraft parts acquired through a Canadian maintenance company."

This wasn't what Harry wanted to hear. "Did your reliable source happen to mention the name of the company?"

"No. But he might also have said something about a drone with weapons capabilities being delivered to a shipbuilding company that's connected to a Canadian ex-pat with Dutch citizenship. That same ex-pat was on friendly terms with the missing businessman."

The ex-pat in question would be Bernard Vanderloord. Had to be. There weren't that many Canadians with his kind of connections. He'd been out of the Netherlands, so Lies hadn't yet met him, but Harry had received an invitation to an opening night at a local theater and Vanderloord was supposed to attend.

He guessed this meant it was time to introduce them.

"Why are you telling me this?" he asked Lars.

"Because a nuclear physicist who once did work for my department, and who I considered a friend—although granted, not a close one—died in London a few weeks ago. The official word is that he had an undiagnosed heart condition." Lars's troubled eyes met Harry's. "The last time I saw him, he seemed very healthy. Coincidentally, he was also working on outfitting drones—built in Canada—with nuclear weapons. I thought you might find the information interesting."

He did. Who would want a nuclear physicist arming a Canadian-manufactured drone dead? Where were those drones ending up?

The real question, Harry decided, wasn't who was buying the drones, but rather, who was pocketing the money from the sale. His willingness to introduce Lies to Vanderloord took an uneasy, downward turn. He didn't care what her job was. It didn't feel right to throw a young woman into this kind of mess, especially since John Carmichael hadn't known about the dead nuclear physicist and his connections to Canada and the Netherlands when he'd assigned her to the Canadian embassy.

Or maybe he had and Harry was being naïve. John ran a spy agency, not a temp service, and Lies wasn't a secretary. He couldn't ignore what he'd just been told. He'd have to pass this information on to her.

The conversation between the two men shifted to the world cycling championships.

An hour after that, Harry closed the door to his flat behind his friend. He reclaimed his chair by the living room window and stared out across the city, the night sky sparkling with lights. His thoughts immediately returned to Lies.

She was a flirt. Also easily bored, and it seemed she'd decided he was her entertainment of choice. She found dozens of little ways to get under his skin. Yet she did every mundane task he tossed her way with a careful attention to detail, as if her career in the diplomatic services rested on her ability to reconcile his credit card statements. He'd taken her to seven embassy functions so far and at each one she'd maintained her cover with ease. Everyone who'd met her accepted her as the well-meaning but very entitled daughter of a diplomat. As far as he could tell, he was the only one who paid any more than a surface attention to her. He had no reason to think she couldn't do the job her real boss had assigned her.

But her becoming involved with Vanderloord was more dangerous than he'd suspected, or led CSIS to believe. Alcine had gone back to Italy scared, although she hadn't been able—or willing—to explain why. If Lies didn't already know any of what Lars had just told him, meaning she hadn't been fully informed before accepting this assignment, then she had the right to back out. If she chose to stay, when Harry finally introduced her to Vanderloord he intended to stick close by her side.

He'd brought her here. That made him responsible for her safety.

Monday morning, he called her into his office. She looked tired and he wondered what she'd been up to all weekend. Irritation over the list of possibilities assaulting his imagination made him abrupt. Whatever it was, it must have been fun.

"I'm taking you to dinner," he said. "There are a few things we need to discuss about your performance." That was the code they'd established for anything important they didn't want overheard in the office.

Her blue eyes lit up like those of a cat ready to pounce. She had zero respect for him or his position, especially when they were alone, and he'd learned to be wary of that particular glint in her eye.

She tucked a short, bouncy blond ringlet behind her ear. The diamond studs twinkled. "I'll run home at five o'clock to change and then meet you back here."

He saw no need for her to change. Her plan to do so further triggered alarms. She wore gray leggings and a black-and-gray striped tunic paired with wine-colored leather boots and clunky silver bracelets on both slender wrists. "What you have on is fine."

"You've got to be kidding. My father would have a heart attack if I went out for a business dinner dressed like this."

Whenever she brought up the fictitious father he knew he was in trouble. Yet in spite of it he was intrigued, curious to see where she was headed. "I thought we'd go somewhere casual."

"I don't believe you know what that word means." She perched on the corner of his desk, making herself comfortable and him infinitely less so. "Tell you what. If you come by my flat around seven, I'll cook dinner for you instead."

Harry wasn't especially great at witty repartee, but this one had been handed to him. "You can cook?"

She shrugged, a light lifting of one shoulder. "How hard can it be?" He had no quick comeback for that and she laughed. "Relax, Harry. Yes, I can cook. We're having steaks. You can bring a bottle of wine if you like. I won't have anything that's up to your standards."

Dinner in private with a beautiful woman who worked for him would be inappropriate, and under normal circumstances he'd never suggest it. But, considering the conversation they needed to have, it might be for the best. Still, letting her get her own way entirely wasn't a safe thing to do.

"I'm not a wine snob." He wasn't a snob at all, or at least he liked to believe that he wasn't, and it annoyed him that she was constantly alluding to it with these little digs. "I wasn't born into money, Lies. I worked for this position." He got in a dig of his own. "The same, I'm sure, as you worked for yours." Since she was currently pretending to be someone whose father had earned her this position, she could hardly rebut.

Lies patted the desk. "In that case, there's no need for you to bother with wine. I have a lovely bottle I picked up at the market." Her lips curved into a bright smile as she stood. "See you at seven."

And with that, Harry decided as the door closed behind her, he'd just lost any advantage he might have held. He drummed his fingertips on his thigh.

He was taking that bottle of wine.

CHAPTER FOUR

THINGS WERE FINALLY PROGRESSING with Vanderloord. No matter how hard she pushed, nothing else would have made Harry agree to come to her place for dinner.

Lies was relieved. The embassy was dull as dirt. She wasn't meant to work in an office day in and day out. Life was too short.

She stopped at the market on her way home to purchase the steaks she'd promised Harry, as well as ready-made salad and a few pastries to go with their post-dinner coffee. Food in the Netherlands was reasonably priced, fresh, and much of it already prepared for convenience. She loaded her purchases into the basket on her bicycle, unlocked it from the bike rack outside of the store, and pedaled home, where she stowed the bicycle in the garage on the main level of her building and took the lift to her floor.

Inside her flat, she dropped her groceries on the marble counter in the tiny kitchen and got to work. The steaks had been pre-marinated and would only take a short time to cook. She set placemats, napkins, and cutlery on a tall bistro table with two high-backed stools that faced sliding windows overlooking the roof garden on the townhouse next door.

The bell rang at two minutes to seven and Lies let Harry in. He'd changed into a sport jacket and jeans and looked very handsome. Casual, too. She took the bottle of wine he handed her and examined the label while she got over the shock.

"It's Canadian," she said.

His grin of smug satisfaction that he'd surprised her gave her insides an odd little rush. When he smiled he wasn't nearly as stuffy.

"I always give out Canadian wines," he said. "We have several excellent wineries and our embassy is here to help promote Canadian businesses internationally."

Lies, recovering, shook her head in mock despair. This sounded more like the Harry she'd come to know. "Congratulations. You've discovered your super power. You turn social engagements into business transactions."

Harry's grin deepened. "And you thought I was a snob."

"That was your word, not mine."

"But you thought it."

"OK, yes I did," Lies admitted, entranced by that smile. This side of Harry was rare. "And I take it back. You aren't a snob. You're a workaholic."

"I prefer to think I'm dedicated. I like to give everything I do one hundred percent of my effort."

The rush in her stomach spread to her toes before reality dug in its heels. Anyone else she'd accuse of flirting with her. Harry, however, meant just what he said.

He shrugged out of his jacket and hung it on a hook by the door. The sleeves of his white cotton shirt had been rolled to the elbow. "Something smells good."

"I promised you steak."

While she finished putting dinner on the table, he uncorked the wine and poured it in glasses. A few minutes later, they were seated across from each other. Harry sliced into his steak. It cut like butter, she was pleased to see. It had been a while since she'd cooked one for anyone else and she'd worried.

"What do you know about a nuclear physicist who died in London a few weeks ago?" he asked.

So much for polite dinner conversation. Of all the things she'd thought he'd bring up, this item hadn't entered the picture. She wasn't sure how much of what she knew was safe to disclose. It depended a great deal on why Harry was suddenly interested. CSIS believed the CIA, or possibly the Israeli Mossad, had targeted the physicist because of his involvement in the development of nuclear weapons. CSIS also believed he'd been helping arm countries that hadn't signed the international Non-Proliferation Treaty.

She set down her knife and fork, laying them carefully along the edge of her plate, then picked up her drink. She eyed him over its rim. "Why do you ask?"

She listened with vigilant attention to details and a growing concern as Harry relayed to her the conversation he'd had with his friend in the Dutch *Kernfysische dienst*. Aircraft parts from Canada, and headed to Russia through the Netherlands, was a serious problem on several levels. The Dutch had initiated trade sanctions against Russia, and overall, relations with Russia remained uneasy throughout Europe. Canada didn't want to find itself caught in the middle, even inadvertently. The trail left by those aircraft parts could lead as easily to Canada as from it, and Bernard Vanderloord, a Canadian national, appeared to be at the hub. Harry, as defense trade commissioner, had a real problem unfolding and she couldn't help him with it other than to relay his information back to her director. CSIS wasn't planning to shut Vanderloord down and she couldn't tell him.

Dan owed her more chocolate.

"No one will blame you if you want to ask for a reassignment and go home," Harry said.

The comment interrupted Lies's train of thought. She'd been frowning at her plate as she'd processed everything he'd told her and what it could mean. "Why on earth would I want to go home?"

"You don't need to be caught up in this. Whatever's going on, it's more dangerous than I led John to believe."

Harry was worried about her. That was both sweet and exasperating. She hadn't gotten her job by being pretty. Or thanks to her rich, fictitious daddy.

"I'm an intelligence officer. There's always going to be an element of danger to the work I do," she replied. "It's part of the game."

"Game?" Harry echoed. His eyebrows rode up his forehead to express incredulity at her choice of words.

"Of course." Treating each case as a game was a disassociation tactic they'd been taught in training and she was good at it. "Sometimes I win, sometimes I lose."

"What happens if you lose a game where the stakes are higher than you expected?"

"If the stakes are high for me, then they're going to be astronomical for the other team. I make sure the odds are in my favor."

"They can't always be."

"And that's what keeps the game exciting." Lies picked at her salad, stirring it around with her fork. "I know you don't get it, Harry. That's why you're on a different career path from me. But I love what I do. And don't expect me to believe that the stakes aren't high in your line of work too."

"Mine don't end up with me dead."

She rolled her eyes at him. "That's melodramatic. I stand a greater chance of dying in a plane crash."

"Tell that to the guy who disappeared while delivering aircraft parts to Russia."

"Transactions of that sort are rarely a secret. There are too many players. My own mother doesn't know what I do. That's the whole 'spy' part of it."

"You've never been caught in the act?"

Michael's face crowded into her thoughts. He hadn't trusted her from the very beginning, but she'd figured that out before she'd gotten in too deep. And he'd never associated her with CSIS. He'd expected her to run to the police and been led to believe that she'd been too scared to do it.

"No," she said. "If you don't have your target's trust then you aren't going to learn anything of real value anyway. On the other hand, if you've earned a high level of trust you aren't likely to lose it. I'll try to earn Vanderloord's trust. I either will or I won't. He, however, will never have mine and that gives me the advantage."

Harry's brown eyes continued to radiate doubt. "Vanderloord's been operating a long time. I doubt if he's trusted anyone in years."

"I'm not after the keys to his safe, Harry. I don't need to catch him red-handed with stolen aircraft parts in the back of his truck either. I have to figure out how his network operates so it can be dismantled. I'll pay attention to where he goes and the people he talks to. He has his sights on you and I want to know why. Since I have access to you, and to the same information you do at the embassy, I'm already two steps closer to what he wants than he is."

"What about the dead nuclear physicist?"

"Who's to say he didn't really die of a pre-existing, undiagnosed heart condition?" Lies countered. If the defense minister was somehow involved in that, her boss would have a stroke.

Harry attacked his steak with his fork and knife. "I don't like any of this. I should never have gone to John."

Lies longed to ask if it would make any difference to him if she were a man, but she already knew the answer, so why start a fight?

"When will I meet Vanderloord?" she asked instead.

The small living area of the flat had darkened with the slow, dwindling twilight. Landscape lighting in the rooftop garden next door flickered on, illuminating manicured shrubs, as well as the table where Lies and Harry were sitting.

He swallowed a bite of steak. "Wednesday night. There's a theater opening that embassy staff have been invited to. I believe a few of the performers are Canadian and they're hoping a large Canadian presence will help with promotion."

A night at the theater was on par with a trip to the dentist. "Don't you people ever get invited to anything fun?"

"The Dutch aren't as enthusiastic about truck pulls as you are," Harry replied. "But the next soccer match tickets are yours." He shifted the subject. "What do you do for entertainment? Give me an example. Tell me about your weekend."

"I helped my cousin paint her living room." And OK yes, she spotted the irony.

So did Harry. His mouth twitched at the corners. "How disappointing that I don't have fun social engagements like that on my calendar."

"There was dancing involved." She twirled a finger. "Oh, yes. And a criminal element."

"I'd be disappointed if there weren't. Let's hear the details."

She told him about Baart and the restaurant, although she left out Yasmin's part in it.

"You could tell he was involved in criminal activity simply by looking around?" Harry sounded skeptical. "Isn't that called jumping to conclusions?"

"I'm a trained observer, specializing in money laundering." It was why she was here, she could have reminded him. "When a restaurant's tables are busy, but no one touches the cash register all evening except to take money out, something is definitely wrong."

"Fair enough, although I doubt it would stand up in court. How does the dancing fit in?"

"There's a nightclub next door to the restaurant."

"Of course there is. Did they need their walls painted too?"

Lies laughed. He had a good sense of humor, quiet and dry, if one listened for it.

They finished their dinner and the bottle of wine. Harry helped her clear the table, carrying the dishes to the kitchen sink. She started the coffeemaker, amazed he hadn't yet made up some excuse to leave.

She turned around and bumped into him. "Whoops. The kitchen's a bit small."

He didn't move. "On Wednesday, how are you planning to meet Vanderloord? Do you want me to introduce you?"

"There are dozens of ways for me to meet him on my own. I can bump into him by accident, like this..." She smiled at Harry, who was still standing too close, and gestured between them, but he didn't back off. "Or I could follow him to the men's room and offer to buy him a drink. Maybe ask him if he has a spare fifty euros so I can show him a good time."

Harry's expression darkened. "Be careful, Lies."

"Relax. I'll start a conversation the way any normal person would in a similar situation. I'll ask him what he thinks of the performance and we can take it from there."

"I'll introduce you. I want to know what's going on."

She liked that Harry was a gentleman throwback to another generation. It set him apart. She enjoyed having him pull out her chair and open doors for her too. Every woman liked being made to feel special.

But not when it came to her job.

"This isn't embassy business," she reminded him.

He was undeterred, brushing off her objections as if she hadn't spoken. "We're going back to Plan A. I'm pursuing you. It gives me an excuse to stay close so I can help if you need it."

"I've already got Plan B established. No one at the embassy is going to believe your sudden interest in me."

"No?" The look he gave her made the already small room shrink to a mere postage-stamp size. He tugged at one of her curls, rolling it between his thumb and forefinger. "I'm single and I like beautiful women as much as the next man."

He was playing her game with her in order to get his own way. She could hardly complain about the tactics he used, but she preferred honesty from him. While not completely predictable, he was one hundred percent dependable. She trusted him because of it.

And that gave him the advantage, because he certainly did not trust her in return.

All she could do to retaliate was call his bluff. She stepped in close, placing her hand on his chest. It was solid, like he was, and warm beneath the crisp cotton fabric of his shirt. Her palm prickled with heat. He was only an inch or so taller than she. If she'd been wearing heels, she'd have at least one advantage over him. She met his gaze and read interest. Her breathing quickened, leaving her head spinning. He really did find her attractive. There was an advantage for her in that too.

He had the most beautiful mouth, the lower lip slightly fuller than the top. It was generous and firm, the color of raspberries in early August. She'd have one little taste. Then he'd call a halt, conceding Plan A was ridiculous.

She pressed her mouth to his, nipping that full lower lip between both of hers and gently tugging. She stroked it with the tip of her tongue. He tasted delicious. Her heart began pounding. A sizzle of heat shot through her belly. Caution kicked up a ruckus inside her head, letting her know in no uncertain terms that she'd made an error in judgment. In this one area, he wasn't trustworthy.

Not in the least.

Rather than draw back to neutral territory and regroup, as she should, she threw herself on a landmine. She slid her arms around his neck. His hands came to rest on her back, crushing her breasts to his ribs. A knee nudged her thighs apart. His tongue brushed against hers and her legs threatened to collapse. Harry, far from passive, could kiss.

The coffeemaker coughed, spitting the last of the hot water through the filter to signal the end of its cycle, interrupting the moment. Harry's hands slid down her back to her hips. He lifted his head, his expression as steady and serious as always.

He had nerves of steel.

"I'll introduce you to Vanderloord during intermission," he said, as if the matter were settled. Lies, bemused, couldn't find the right words to argue. He'd proven his point. Her mind was a blank. He eased her aside, his fingers gently biting into her skin before they released her, and slid past her to get to the counter. "You see to the coffee. I'll carry the pastries."

She was filling two mugs with the dark, steaming brew before it struck her that this was her home, not his, and they weren't at the office pretending he was her boss, and she didn't have to do everything he said.

Her scattered thoughts finally returned. If he'd been at all smug about his victory she'd be fuming right now. But Harry, true to his nature, didn't seem to realize he'd won anything of significance. He'd only stated what, to him, was a practical solution to a problem that weighed on his mind.

Meaning they were back to Plan A.

Again, she found herself in a position that forced her to pick her battles. And again, when she got down to it, it wasn't worth fighting. She'd been the one to assure him there was no danger. Plan A and Plan B were both his to begin with, and could be easily adapted.

So what did it matter which one they used?

For the sake of politeness, and so Harry wouldn't give away how much that kiss had scrambled his brain, he'd stayed long enough to drink his coffee. What they'd talked about he couldn't recall, only that Lies had been subdued and probably plotting how best to use the incident against him.

He'd tossed and turned the rest of the night, unable to sleep as he'd contemplated where he went wrong. Probably when he'd developed an uncontrollable urge to touch one of those intriguing blond ringlets to see if it was as silky as it appeared. Up until they'd entered the kitchen Harry could have sworn he'd been holding his own.

Wednesday night, as he fastened his black cummerbund and knotted his thistle bowtie in preparation for the theater, he was still on edge. Vanderloord was a handsome man. Harry was not. He couldn't help but wonder how Lies might compare them. Whereas Vanderloord was tall, fair-haired, and spent a great deal of time at the gym to stave off signs of aging, Harry was stocky, dark-headed, and willing to let time take its toll. He preferred healthy living to turning back time. He was average at best.

Despite that, he'd never had difficulty with women. They didn't throw themselves at his feet, but they didn't run away screaming either. Alcine had been beautiful, even more so than Lies, if one examined the two women critically and judged solely on appearance.

Yet he'd found Alcine as dull as she'd deemed him. She'd enjoyed going to social functions with him, and he'd appreciated her knack for putting people at ease, but any spark there'd been between them had fizzled a long time ago. The only difference was that he'd felt no need to tell her so to her face. At least when she'd figured out that Vanderloord was more interested in Harry than her she'd been decent enough to warn him before fleeing back to Italy.

He fastened his cufflinks. There were no sparks with Lies either. These were violent explosions. He was attracted to her, but he pitied the man who became involved with her for real. If it were him, he'd never be able to dismiss her sharing such a kiss with another man as part of her job, whereas she seemed to take it in stride.

There had to be better ways for Lies to approach Vanderloord than by feigning attraction. She was playing with fire.

So was Harry. He had to pretend he was pretending to be attracted to her. She made him feel tired.

And also alive.

He donned his tuxedo jacket and headed off to the theater.

When he got there, Lies had already arrived.

His eyes immediately singled her out from the throng waiting in the reception area for the doors to open and the performance to start. The dress she wore was stunning, long and black and formfitting. Two bands of fabric cupped her shoulders to hold it in place. It was cut very low in front and high at the thighs, and tiny threads of silver shimmered all over the front skirt panel when she moved. The mass of blond ringlets had been pinned up, emphasizing the blueness of her eyes and the angle of her cheekbones.

Harry pretended not to see the people trying to attract his attention as he cut through the crowd to her side.

Awareness flashed in her eyes when she saw who had joined her, heartening him, before her expression smoothed and the mask dropped into place. Their game was that he was attracted to her but she didn't share his feelings—not really such a hard thing to pull off, considering how close it was to the truth.

The game became hardest for him when they were alone together. For the past two days he'd made certain they weren't and she'd been unusually cooperative about it.

He didn't recognize the older couple she spoke with. She introduced them to him. They were Canadians, parents of one of the performers, and here on vacation. Harry chatted politely with them, the whole time very conscious of Lies. He couldn't fault her professionalism in public. She preferred to torment him in private.

Out of the corner of his eye, Harry watched Bernard Vanderloord descend the few steps from the foyer to the reception area and disappear into the crowd. It became that much more difficult to remember he wasn't to interfere. Even before Alcine and the Albanian ambassador's wife, he'd disliked Vanderloord for the same reason most people appeared to enjoy his company. He was too polished. Too smooth. He had secrets behind that veneer.

As long as Lies did nothing rash, Harry would do his best to keep his nose out of her investigation. He'd allow her to do her job. But he wasn't going to be left in a position of guilt if something happened to her that he could have prevented.

The lights in the room flickered, signaling the performance was about to begin, and the doors opened wide. People trickled toward them in a wave that turned into a tide. Harry extended an elbow to Lies. Their tickets had them seated in the same row, although not together.

The play was good. His mind wasn't on it however. He couldn't have sworn to the plot. He stood at intermission and waited in the aisle for Lies so he could accompany her to the reception area.

"Are you enjoying yourself?" he asked.

"I'm having a lovely time." Her smile underscored a blatant insincerity. "I haven't forgotten about those soccer tickets you promised me."

He had to fight to hide his amusement so as not to encourage her. "Let's head to the bar."

She wore high heels, giving her an inch of height over him, which was good. Anyone looking for him would see her first. Vanderloord, who rarely missed an opportunity to speak with him, couldn't possibly miss that they were together.

The queue at the bar stretched the length of the room but moved quickly.

Harry quietly drew Lies's attention to her objective. "There he is. Third person on the right, holding the glass with the lime." Vanderloord had seen them too. Harry caught the arrested stillness to him before he returned his focus to his companions and their conversation. "Stay here while I get our drinks. He won't approach me until we're together. It would be rude for me to walk away and abandon you with a man you don't know, so it gives him a guaranteed audience."

"Club soda for me, please," she said.

He took that as acquiescence.

As he made his way through the queue his plan slowly unraveled. Intermission was only twenty minutes long and a number of other people also wanted to speak with him. Also, he'd overestimated Lies's willingness to follow his lead. He should have known she wasn't about to pass up her first opportunity to meet her objective. When the people Vanderloord had been speaking with moved on and she saw that he was alone, and Harry had been sidelined, she took matters into her own hands.

Harry watched in helpless frustration as she walked over to Vanderloord and introduced herself.

CHAPTER FIVE

AWARENESS CHASED UP LIES'S spine, then settled between her shoulder blades in a subliminal message that she was being watched. A quick, side-eyed glance Harry's way said she was right and that he was annoyed.

So was she.

Not, however, with him, but herself. This inexplicable attraction toward someone who was hardly her type had caught her unawares, but when it came to mixing business with pleasure, she really had learned her lesson. Kissing Harry had crossed a line and created a complication she'd need to address before it got out of hand. Therefore, rule number one moving forward was going to be simple—no kissing anyone even remotely connected to any investigation, no matter how attractive or intriguing she might find them.

Bernard Vanderloord proved to be a little of both.

If Lies hadn't known he was forty-seven years old, she'd have placed him a full decade younger. He had a commanding presence and a hint of ruthlessness to him, no doubt about that. He was broad-chested and tall, an inch or two over six feet, with the long, lean limbs his Dutch countrymen made famous. He wore his bleached blond hair short and heavily gelled. He had a wide mouth, angular cheeks and a sharply bladed nose. His eyes were a clear, brilliant blue in a lightly-tanned face.

Right now those sharp eyes, which said he missed very little, were fixated on her in a manner both bold and assessing. This was a man who pursued his goals with single-minded focus. She couldn't wait to find out more about him. He'd make an excellent diversion from Harry.

"Good evening," she said, extending her hand. "We haven't met. My name is Marlies Wiersma and I'm new with the Canadian embassy. I couldn't help noticing that you speak English. Mr. Jordan suggested I introduce myself to as many Canadians as possible this evening, and from your accent, either you're from Canada or you grew up there."

"Bernard Vanderloord. You have a good ear," he congratulated her. "My parents moved to Canada when I was a small child." He held her hand a few seconds too long, although not long enough to be awkward, more as if he'd already sized her up and found something puzzling about her. He was good. "Wiersma," he echoed, repeating her surname with its proper pronunciation. "I'm going to guess that your background is Frisian."

If what Harry said about the Albanian diplomat's wife was true, Vanderloord preferred bored wives on the lookout for a distraction. When the diplomat's wife developed too many expectations, he'd cut her loose.

Lies could play at being bored, self-absorbed, and uninterested in long-term commitments. "It is," she said in reply to Vanderloord's comment regarding her background. "I still have family in the Netherlands, although I was born in Ontario."

"Is that what attracted you to work with the embassy here?"

Lies laughed. "Heavens, no. The Netherlands is like home to me. I might as well have stayed in Canada. I was offered this position temporarily because I speak both Dutch and Frisian. Hopefully I'll only be here a few months until something more exciting comes along. I'd requested Paris, but I don't know enough French." Harry, or someone else, could tell him she'd gotten this position through her diplomat father. She didn't need to give everything away right off the bat. And she'd lied about not speaking French because it might come in handy. Most CSIS agents were fluent in Canada's second official language. She prattled on. "What brought you back to the Netherlands? Do you have family here too?"

"No family, I'm afraid. My business is based here." He was quick to change the subject. "How are you enjoying the performance?"

She'd seen none of it. All she'd been aware of was Harry sitting close by and the problem he posed. She threw his name out to see how Vanderloord would react to it. "Harry assures me it's very good."

Amusement softened the harsh lines of Vanderloord's mouth. "I take it the theater isn't a passion of yours?"

"I'm more of a Tiësto fan," she confessed cheerfully, naming a famous Dutch DJ she did, in fact, like very much.

Vanderloord placed a hand to his chest as if feigning a heart attack. "Electronic dance music. Thank you for making me feel every one of my years."

He was testing her to see how she'd react to the difference in age between them and she accepted it as an invitation to flirt. "Age is a state of mind. I like to dance. It doesn't have to be to electronic music, although the energy behind it is very contagious." She widened her eyes, exaggerating her enthusiasm. "You should try it sometime."

A laugh muscle flinched in his cheek. "Who says I've never tried it?"

"Have you?"

"No. I value my hearing more than you obviously do."

His amusement with her had shifted to interest, exactly the reaction she'd hoped for from him, but she was careful not to pursue her flirting any further than this. She didn't know enough about him yet and would hate to make a misstep so early in the game. Besides, he'd have to work for it if he planned to use her to get to Harry. Let him think it was his idea, not hers.

They chatted for a few more minutes before they both moved on to other guests.

She was disentangling herself from a retired civil servant with a penchant for touching when Harry finally rejoined her. While he was far too circumspect to give away his feelings in public, his displeasure was evident in his coolness toward her as he handed over the club soda she'd requested.

He had the exact opposite effect on her than the one he'd intended. Her skin flushed with warmth under his silent censure. Her heart, steady throughout her conversation with Vanderloord, chose now to exhibit erratic behavior. The advantage continued to go to Harry.

She couldn't have that.

The lights flickered, indicating the show was about to recommence, saving her from having to engage him in small talk. She took a long sip of her drink, then discarded it on a nearby side table before preceding him into the theater.

The second half of the show, much like the first, was interminable. Harry remained transfixed by the performance on stage. When the lights finally came on, Lies was ecstatic. They hadn't been invited to the cast party afterwards, meaning for them the evening was over, which was fine with her too. She'd gotten the introduction to Vanderloord she came for.

She and Harry became separated in the crowd at the door. Lies didn't wait for him but made her way out to the street. Her dress meant riding a bicycle was impractical so she'd planned to take a taxi home.

She had her cellphone in her hand and was preparing to call for service when Harry reappeared.

"I'll drive you home," he said.

His tone indicated this was one of those times she should choose her battles with care. Besides she was tired, and the thought of waiting for a taxi late at night in these shoes held zero appeal.

She walked with him to his car, gripping his arm because of her heels. Harry unlocked the car door, and without a word, held it open for her. She smoothed her skirt underneath her as she slid into the passenger seat. He walked around the hood and got in behind the wheel. His continued silence picked away at her nerves.

Since he could remain quiet far longer than she'd ever manage, she didn't bother to try and compete. "You were trapped and I had to do something. I told him you'd asked me to introduce myself to fellow Canadians," she said.

"That was quick thinking."

His neutral tone belied the sincerity of his praise. But she'd already decided that fighting with him was counterproductive, and if she wanted to change her strategy, they'd be better off working as a team. To do that they had to be honest with each other and Harry was holding back information. What he'd told her about Vanderloord's interest in him didn't bear weight. She'd brought Harry's name into their conversation and gotten little to no reaction beyond what she'd expect from someone pursuing business opportunities, legal or otherwise. Harry's distaste for the other man was what confused her most.

She took a shot in the dark. "Why are you so obsessed with the fact that Vanderloord is trying to get close to you? I know it's partly because of your position with the embassy and your contacts in National Defence, but you're paid to cater to people like him and of course he'd try and take advantage of that. It's what businessmen do. To me, your dislike of him seems a little too personal."

Harry tapped his thumb on the steering wheel as he stared straight ahead through the windshield. A crowd of teenagers swept past the parked car while Lies waited for him to frame a response.

Despite what Harry believed, this neighborhood was no safer than the one CSIS had picked as a base for its operations. One boy had a gang tattoo climbing up his neck to his jaw. She could see it by the light of the street lamps, ugly and crude, obviously done by an amateur. He'd regret that in a few years, assuming he didn't already. Another boy had what looked like a knife in his right front jeans pocket. The outline was visible, and yet another reason she was glad she'd accepted Harry's offer of a ride. She liked the diamond studs in her ear and preferred to keep them.

"He was the reason Alcine and I broke up," Harry said.

Her attention snapped back to him. She vaguely recalled him once mentioning that he'd recently split with his girlfriend. He'd seemed over it at the time and so she'd forgotten about it. A tiny spark of jealousy—as unwanted as it was unexpected—flared that it continued to bother him. There was only one reason it could irritate Harry so much.

"She cheated on you." He said nothing and she knew

she'd guessed right. He was honest by nature and he'd insist on it from the people closest to him. Her jealousy flipped to indignation on his behalf and unease on hers. She dallied with the truth every day, stretching its limits and rearranging boundaries. "You deserve better."

The pad of his thumb continued to drum against the leather steering wheel. "She thought she did too."

"I take it her relationship with Vanderloord didn't last."

"Alcine came to warn me when he began expressing too much interest in my connections at the trade commission and the embassy. She's been around diplomatic circles long enough to know which types of questions are inappropriate."

"And yet she didn't know it's also inappropriate to begin a new relationship before ending a current one?"

She needed to dial her indignation back a notch. She had no business being this invested in his private life. Not when she was in no position to cast stones.

"That doesn't mean she's a terrible person or we can't remain friends. We really weren't suited, Lies. If it hadn't been Vanderloord it would have been someone else. I don't have to like it though. Or him."

"Do you still love her?" Lies asked. The question was nosy and none of her business, but it was important. She couldn't imagine Harry, of all people, being able to kiss her the way he had if he harbored unresolved feelings for another woman. While she'd underestimated him in some areas, she refused to believe she'd misjudged him.

"No," he said. "I don't think I ever did. She didn't love me either."

The level of relief that washed through her was unwarranted and she chose not to examine it. "How long were you together?"

"Three years."

"Three *years*?" Lies tried to wrap her head around that. "And you didn't love each other? Not even in the beginning?"

Harry shrugged, as if to say he couldn't be certain, and what did it matter?

"Have you ever been in love?" he countered.

"Lots of times." She began ticking them off on her fingers. "Timmy Bryant in kindergarten. He had these adorable dreadlocks. Louis Anders in grade three. His eyelashes touched his eyebrows. Mr. Humphries in third period English my junior year, although in fairness to him, that was one-sided. He was the soul of propriety." Not unlike Harry. She hastened past that. "Pete in grade twelve. He broke my heart. I slowed down in college and spent more time on my studies and career. There was James my fourth year, and then no one until—"

Damn. She should have stopped at James.

"Until?"

"Never mind."

Thankfully, he didn't pursue it. "My point is," he continued, "you understand how subjective and fleeting love can be. There's the initial attraction stage, then building the relationship. You start to talk about a future together. Then you enter the honesty stage, and from there, you move on to stability. Alcine and I were never really honest with each other. Things began to go stale whenever we talked about our futures. They never aligned. And rather than confront the problem we ignored it. Our relationship was doomed from the beginning."

"That's a very scientific approach to choosing a life partner," Lies said. "I can't imagine why she wasn't swept off her feet."

"Care to tell me why this 'until' of yours was so

different? At what stage did you two part ways?" His expression changed, as if an unpleasant thought had intruded. "Unless you're still together."

"We're not." Lies hesitated. Harry, who possessed an acute sense of right and wrong, could be judgmental and she wasn't sure how much she was willing to tell him. The man she thought she'd loved had been a role Michael played. It had been painful enough having to admit to her bosses that she'd gotten involved with someone who'd never really existed. "That honesty stage you speak of should probably come first."

Tension seeped into the confines of the car. "You got involved with someone you were investigating."

Her stomach plunged. "John told you."

"He didn't have to. You aren't as mysterious as you think. It's obvious you like to test boundaries." Then, Harry surprised her. "Everyone makes decisions they regret at some point in their lives. But if you never make any decisions, or only choose the safe options, then you aren't really living. To be honest, I envy you. I suppose in some ways, I envy Bernard Vanderloord too. Alcine is only a small part of the reason why he rubs me the wrong way. Maybe not even the real reason at all."

Lies had wanted the truth from him and he'd given it to her. More of it than she'd expected him to. She owed him something in return. It all boiled down to whether or not she trusted him with something so personal, and Harry being who he was, she didn't see any harm.

"I wasn't investigating Michael, although he was part of the operation. I took an entry-level position at a company owned by an uncle of his who was suspected of laundering drug money from western Mexico. Once I was in place, I arranged to bump into Michael in a bar CSIS knew he spent time at. He took the bait exactly the way he was supposed to. We started dating." Her hands had grown cold. She folded them on her lap. This wasn't a story she was proud of. "Unfortunately, I got a lot more invested in our relationship than he did. It turns out he was good at faking those stages of love."

"John sent you here to get you back in the saddle." Harry said it as if he'd made a brilliant discovery. "That's why he wouldn't send someone else."

"I *knew* you asked him to replace me."

"Of course I did. I'm not in the habit of prostituting women in exchange for information."

She knew so few gentlemen in her line of work. Harry was a baseline for morality. She liked that about him, even if it proved inconvenient at times.

"Neither is CSIS. There are, however, some cases better suited to women than men. And vice versa. There's also an agent's background to consider. You forget that I speak the languages here. Not many intelligence officers do."

He had no argument for that. He faced her more fully, the frown in his eyes expressing the depth of his concern over the entire situation. "So do your job in a way that won't have me worrying you might be in danger."

He'd make a terrible agent. He was too protective. Too disapproving. He'd give too much away. And yet she was charmed.

"*We* can start by being upfront with each other," she said. By each other she meant him, but he didn't need to know that. "I can't tell you what I learn from Vanderloord, but I can say where I'm going to be when I'm with him. In return, you're going to have to let go of the notion you're somehow responsible for me."

He shifted in his seat, shrinking the small space between them another few inches, reminding Lies of the kiss they'd shared in her kitchen, and that while Harry might not be cut out for intrigue, on the whole his nerves were just fine. What was easier to forget was her resolve. She wanted to kiss him again.

Rather, she wanted him to kiss her. He couldn't possibly understand that the real danger she faced wasn't from Bernard Vanderloord.

She didn't understand this attraction to him herself.

His frustration with Lies and her games made him foolish.

He shouldn't have told her about Alcine. They weren't potential lovers, exchanging past sexual histories. And this wasn't information he wanted to show up in some CSIS file to be scrutinized by strangers, then saved for future exchange in case it proved useful someday.

It wasn't only frustration addling his brain. Everything about her was so at odds with her profession. Her age. Her gender. She could pass for a schoolteacher or an athlete. Her face was mobile, its expressions easily readable.

But in reality the expressiveness was all an act, each lift of her brow or tilt of her chin carefully calculated to convey any meaning she wished. Despite the mistake she'd made with the mysterious Michael, Harry had no doubt she was good at her job. He'd watched her open, casual friendliness with Vanderloord and would never have believed she was the same woman who took such pleasure in goading him to this level of unrelenting sexual awareness. Awareness crackled between them. There was nothing casual or friendly about it.

He wasn't letting go of his responsibility for her. He'd feel the same way about anyone he'd brought into this situation. She was no different to him. He didn't have the kind of patience it would require to become too involved. "Don't forget that Plan A means I have a vested interest in you."

"Only in public."

Her hands resided on her lap. She'd turned her upper torso toward him while speaking, causing the daring neckline of her gown to slip aside and reveal a fair amount of pale, smooth breast. Her large, thick-lashed eyes, their crystalline blueness masked by shadows, fixed on his face. More specifically, his mouth. They said she hadn't forgotten that kiss either.

Now he could think of nothing else.

"Playing a part isn't as easy for me," he confessed. "I can't simply flip a switch and pretend to care one minute but not the next."

She didn't try to use his dilemma against him, preying on his weakness, as he'd come to expect. If anything she seemed sympathetic.

"It's never easy," she said. "At least it shouldn't be. It takes training and practice. That's why it's a game."

Harry worked in business and politics so he was well used to games. He hated to think how far she'd go to win the one she was playing with Vanderloord. She claimed the man she'd fallen for, this Michael, hadn't been under investigation, but that he'd been a part of it told Harry the boundaries she operated under could become very blurred in her mind.

His were better defined.

And yet, even though he hated games of this sort and she was a player, he still wanted to kiss her again, which spoke volumes about him and his own strength of character—none of it flattering. A month ago, before he'd found out about Vanderloord's activities, he would have walked away from a woman like Lies.

Now, after having Lies thrust on him against his will?

He'd begin a game of his own. His would be more direct. She could use the reminder that, if she planned to pursue men like Vanderloord, at least one of her boundaries should be inflexible. Sympathy was about to become her mistake. She believed him trustworthy.

Well, he was a man too.

He slung an elbow over the back of his seat, allowing the knuckles of his dangling fingers to gently stroke the smooth skin of her naked upper arm. His gaze dropped to her partially exposed breast, remained for a second, then flicked back to her face.

She went very still. Her eyes turned to pools of blue ice. "I didn't mean for you to practice on me."

They were sitting in his car on a side street in the hub of the city. Although it was late at night, and the street deserted, privacy was hardly assured. Nevertheless, he tossed down the gauntlet. "You can stop me anytime you like."

"Nobody's stopping you."

She sounded so complacent. So confident she'd best him. He almost relented. Instead, he tracked the tips of his fingers along the length of her shoulder to the base of her throat, then upward to her jaw. The pulse leaped beneath his light touch and he was glad he'd persisted. Some responses couldn't be feigned. He tucked the crook of his finger beneath her chin and angled it upward, bringing her mouth more in line with his. Seated, without the advantage of heels, she wasn't nearly as tall.

He bent forward, pressing his lips to hers. He eased his right hand behind her head and placed his left hand on her hip, tugging her body slightly toward him. If not for the stick shift and console between them, she'd be on his lap. He skimmed his hand lower to the top of her thigh, then beneath the whisper-thin fabric of her dress until his palm cupped bare flesh. He felt the sharp inhale of her breath, then caught its soft, fluttering release as she exhaled. Her arm slid beneath his jacket, curled around his waist, and her fingers dipped beneath the band of his trousers at the small of his back.

Excitement coursed through him, exchanging coherent thought for a mixture of base sensations—the scent of her hair. The taste of her skin. The touch of her hands and lips. She'd closed her eyes. He took a second to admire her lovely face, and to try and decipher her expressions, hoping to find a trace of the real Lies in an unguarded moment. Her lashes fluttered apart. Her eyes, filled with a mixture of challenge, trust, and an unmistakable heat, gazed into his. When would she call a halt? How far was she willing to go?

Because he had no plans to end this. Not yet.

He trailed his mouth down the side of her throat, nipping with his teeth and making her gasp, then touching the tip of his tongue to the vee at its base, waiting for her to say *enough*. He squeezed her thigh with his fingers, a light touch of warning, before inching them upward to the tiny scrap of fabric covering her mound. He ran his thumb over the triangle, testing the spring of tight curls pinned beneath it. Her fingers fisted against his back. Her other hand clutched at the front of his shirt and she arched her hips, inviting a more intimate touch. Desire exploded at the front of his skull. He lowered his mouth to the gap where her dress had exposed part of her breast, nudging it open, and the soft moan of pleasure that escaped her as his mouth found her nipple, teasing it with his tongue, was all the encouragement he needed to ignore that this was a game and what he was doing crossed every single one of his boundaries.

At the edge of incoherent, desire-driven thought, his conscience rapped sharply. Despite all her confident talk of past boyfriends, it was painfully obvious that Lies was far less experienced than he. He was the one going too far.

And on a public side street no less.

A palm beat on the windshield. Harry lifted his head as a blurry face appeared in the steamed-up passenger window, jeering at him. It was one of the young thugs who'd passed the car a short time ago. Behind the boy, three of his friends issued catcalls of encouragement, obviously enjoying the peepshow Harry and Lies were providing.

He withdrew his hand from the slit of Lies's skirt, and straightened the fabric over her breast and thigh with a calm nonchalance he was far from feeling. He ignored the aching strain of his groin as he reached for the ignition and started the engine.

Then coolly, as if being caught making out in his car with a beautiful woman was an everyday occurrence for him, he flipped the laughing boys his middle finger before pulling away from the curb.

CHAPTER SIX

A PAIR OF TICKETS had been left on Lies's desk along with a note:

You said you were a fan. Please enjoy the tickets. Bernard V.

Lies picked up the tickets and examined them. Tiësto. They were for the VIP area at a concert on the upcoming weekend that had been sold out weeks ago. As she held them, wondering what their purpose was, her phone rang.

It was Vanderloord.

"Thank you for the tickets," Lies said, cautious as to how flirtatious to be. The age difference between them was enough that she had to be careful. She'd gotten the impression that Vanderloord liked younger women who posed a challenge. "Is the second one yours?"

"While I would very much enjoy your company," he said wryly, "I can think of a thousand better ways to do so. Take someone your own age. I prefer concerts where there are actual performers and musical instruments."

"Like a harp and violin?" she dared to tease, testing him.

"At the very least a piano."

He definitely had a sense of humor. She liked that. It

was easier to work with. "If I'm ever given tickets to the opera, they're yours." But these tickets weren't a gift and she was curious as to what their price tag would be. He wanted to find out how easily she could be bought and she didn't plan to sell out too cheap. "Is there anything I can help you with?"

"I'd like to book an appointment with Harry," Vanderloord said, getting straight down to business.

She turned into Harry's personal assistant, brisk and polite. "May I ask what it's regarding?"

"There's a Canadian shipping contract about to be put out to tender by DND. I'm interested in obtaining the names of potential second-tier suppliers and Harry should have some knowledge of them."

DND was the Canadian Department of National Defence and the request was nothing out of the ordinary. Unfortunately, Harry's schedule was legitimately booked solid. Lies made an executive decision. This meeting with Vanderloord took precedence over trade commission business, but she couldn't make it too obvious.

"Harry can give you a half hour on Friday, but it'll have to be during lunch." She'd order in sandwiches.

"Whatever is convenient for him."

She hung up, then sat at her desk without moving. She should go talk to Harry and tell him what she'd done to his schedule. He'd been avoiding her for a week now, speaking only when necessary while they waited for Vanderloord to make the next move, which he just had. Harry couldn't ignore her any longer.

She nudged a pen on her desk with her finger. The drive home from the theater that night had been so incredibly awkward and silent. She regretted her part in it—not because she'd encouraged Harry to touch her, but because she had let things go too far. She'd been curious to see if the attraction between them was real or one-sided. Maybe she'd also needed to feed her ego. The affair with Michael had been a blow to her pride.

She couldn't be certain what Harry was angriest about. It wasn't that they'd been caught making out like a couple of teenagers, although he'd definitely been unhappy about that. There was a stronger possibility that he simply didn't want to be attracted to her. He truly didn't like games—which was one reason why he disliked Bernard Vanderloord so much. And because she was an intelligence officer his prejudices carried over to her, so that might well be it.

But if he was angry because he'd tried to teach her a lesson about the dangers of flirting and she'd refused to give in, then they both owned their behavior and between them, they'd have to figure out how to deal with the fallout. Since Vanderloord had finally reached out there was no time like the present.

Ignoring the mad thud of her heart, she approached Harry's office door. It was open a crack. She poked her head around it, peering inside.

His office was what could best be described as austere. He had framed diplomas and certifications on the walls, nothing else. No family. No photo of the queen. No curtains or blinds at the window. Since they were on the second floor his view consisted mainly of trees and the upper levels of other buildings.

Harry was at his desk, his head bent over his work. He had a frown of intense concentration on his face that made him appear so...cold and remote. At least on the surface. There was a whole lot more to him, and it wasn't cold, despite the shivers it gave her. The coolness was an act. Harry used excellent manners to disguise how he felt.

But when he set those manners aside...

She had a hunch he'd be amazing in bed. Part of her longed to find out. The way he'd kissed her and touched her said it wouldn't take much.

Her team leader, however, had been specific that she was to protect her professional integrity for this particular assignment. Because Harry was connected to her investigation, she'd have to tell the CSIS director—because she was answering to him—about it if she slept with him. She could well imagine how that would look after the last confession she'd had to make. She also had a good idea how Harry would feel having CSIS know he'd slept with one of their intelligence officers. His integrity was important to him too.

So was his dignity, but she had fewer qualms about messing with that.

"Would you like to go to a rave?" she asked.

"God no," he replied, without lifting his eyes from whatever he was writing. "Not even at gunpoint." His hand stilled and his head came up. His eyes narrowed. "Why do you ask?"

She stepped fully into the room and closed the door, leaning against it. "Bernard gave me two tickets to a Tiësto concert." She flashed him a brilliant smile. "I gave him a half hour of your time in exchange."

"It's Bernard now, is it?" Harry continued to regard her. "If your new best friend supplied the tickets, why isn't he going to the concert with you?"

She raised her eyebrows. "You have no idea who Tiësto is, do you?"

"I do know what a rave is. OK, I see your point." He glanced at the schedule she'd programmed into his phone for him and pretended he knew how to read it. *Luddite.* "Where did you manage to find a half hour for a meeting?"

"Friday at lunch. He's coming here and I'm ordering sandwiches for two."

Harry sighed. "Let me guess. He's after a list of second-tier suppliers from that new shipbuilding contract. Better order sandwiches for three. You'll want to sit in."

"I could wire your office," she suggested, mostly in fun. She'd do it, but he'd never agree.

A muscle ticked in his jaw. "You aren't wiring embassy offices. Not mine and not anyone else's."

"Then leave the door open so I can eavesdrop. Unless you can come up with a good explanation for my presence."

He settled back in his chair, the tips of his fingers pressed together. The sight of those long fingers reminded her of the feel of them on her skin. Heat lanced up her spine. He was good with his hands.

Very good.

"My office. My rules. I don't need to make up an excuse," he was saying, bringing her abruptly back to the present. "I'm asking you to join us for lunch. We'll keep it casual."

She bit the inside of her cheek to keep from arguing. His world was so easy for him. Hers was somewhat more complicated in that she often dealt with perceptions rather than rules. In this case his rules wouldn't necessarily align with Vanderloord's perceptions. Vanderloord, who was neck-deep in military theft, might well find it curious as to why Harry's assistant was joining their business meeting. Harry was never that casual.

On the other hand, no one would ever imagine Harry in a parked car on a public street with his hand up her skirt and his mouth on her breast either, so stranger things had happened. Which brought her back to her real purpose for coming into his office.

He'd returned his attention to his work, dismissing her with an abruptness that said she'd been right and it wasn't just her. They were both confused about this attraction between them.

"About the other night," she began.

He set his pen down with careful deliberation. His eyes chilled. "I apologized for that."

He had. Beautifully. Whereas she'd mumbled something incoherent and scrambled from the car, then fled as if from the scene of a crime. Not her finest moment.

"I didn't though. I should have." His brown eyes narrowed a little more, probably suspicious as to what her game was, so she plunged ahead before he could remind her that he was busy. They couldn't work together with all this tension between them. "It's hardly your fault I'm so attracted to you."

That got his attention. "Excuse me?"

"I always go straight for the bad boys. You know… The men with an element of danger? An edginess to them? The women in my family are addicted to the adrenaline rush you give us."

"Just so I understand. You're apologizing to me because you can't control yourself around me? Because I'm edgy and *dangerous*?"

"Exactly. So you can see how Plan A will have to be altered. It will be far more believable if I'm into you rather than you pretending to be into me. I've got truth on my side."

"Because I'm such a…bad boy." He stumbled as he said it, trying hard to keep a straight face. He was very close to a smile, which spurred her on.

"Come on, Harry. Admit it. You were being pretty bad at the time." She canted her head to the side and studied him. "Although one could argue that you were also very, very good."

The tips of his ears turned a dull red. "Why do I suddenly feel like the one who's been violated?"

"See? There's your problem. You're making a big deal out of nothing. Neither one of us has been violated." Lies pushed away from the door. She went to the chair in front of his desk and sat down, crossing her legs. She folded her hands on her knee, swinging the toe of one shoe. "We both got caught up in you proving a point. You think I don't know when to stop, but I assure you, there's a limit to how far I'll go for my country."

His expression hardened again. She'd told him about Michael. It hung between them even though Harry was far too much of a gentleman to bring it up. At least not directly.

"What, exactly, is your limit?" he asked.

He made this so *easy*.

She studied her nails. "It's on a case-by-case basis. And quit being judgmental."

He took offense to that. "I'm not judgmental."

"You most certainly are." It was time to be serious. "I'm not into men whose livelihoods are built on the premise that other people are expendable. There's no gray area in that. No lack of understanding on their part. They can dress it up however they like, but at the end of the day, men like Vanderloord are criminals, not businessmen. That's my limit."

And that was a big part of the reason why Harry appealed to her. When it came to his beliefs about right and wrong, he had no gray areas. No matter how much she provoked him, or what lesson he was trying to teach her, or how carried away they'd both gotten, if she'd made the slightest show of resistance in the car the night of the theater, he would have stopped instantly. Harry was completely trustworthy.

She was the one who was not. She liked flirting with danger. And the danger he represented was to her career.

What did that say about her?

"Why don't we play it by ear?" Harry suggested. "Let people speculate about our relationship? It's not as if they aren't already talking."

He was right. It was obvious there was something between them. The mystery was over who'd instigated it and she didn't have the answer to that.

"Fair enough," she said.

She returned to her desk.

Then she picked up the phone and called Yasmin. Those VIP tickets weren't going to waste.

Most people only cared that Bernard Vanderloord was honest in his business dealings with them. They didn't look past the surface to see what his true agenda might be. He was the type of man Harry despised most.

Pride entered into the equation. This would be their first private, face-to-face meeting since he'd found out about the affair. He was glad Lies would also be in attendance. He could hardly—at least not as the defense trade commissioner—punch the other man in the face.

It would be almost as satisfying to see him end up in jail, his reputation in ruins.

"Why don't you join us?" Harry asked Lies, striving to make the invitation sound spur-of-the-moment and not something they'd choreographed in advance. She'd ushered Vanderloord into his office and was making a

production out of unwrapping the sandwiches and serving
the coffee, taking her time, waiting for him to pick up his
cue, which he'd missed. "There's too much food here for
two people."

She displayed both eagerness and a charming
uncertainty, playing her part much better than he did. Her
gaze slid back and forth between him and Vanderloord. "I
don't want to intrude."

"A beautiful woman is never an intrusion,"
Vanderloord interjected.

Harry clenched his back teeth. Alcine and Dita had
fallen for this nonsense. And if Lies's story about a past
lover was to be believed, she was equally susceptible to
charming men.

The thought of Vanderloord touching Lies in the
same manner he had, even if it was only to help
establish her cover, didn't sit well. There was very little
he could do about it however. He'd have to trust that
she really did know what she was doing and she'd
meant it when she said criminal behavior was where she
drew the line.

"Lies is interested in a career as a foreign services
officer," Harry said. "She's proving to be a good student
and a pleasure to work with."

She pulled up a chair next to Vanderloord's and
balanced her plate of sandwiches on her lap. She'd worn a
loose-fitting dress with a flirty skirt that was so short it
rode indecently far up her long legs when she crossed
them, a fact that hadn't escaped either man's attention.
Her open-toed, leather platform ankle boots showed off
pretty pink nail polish. She'd clipped her blond curls away
from her face and the diamond studs she always wore
glittered on the exposed rim of her ear. Her blue eyes
widened with interest as she listened to the two men

discuss Canadian industrial and regional benefits policies and the requirements for second-tier suppliers. She even asked the occasional question that betrayed her supposed ignorance for the subject matter but also a keenness to learn.

She sounded exactly like a young woman eager to advance her career.

Harry was impressed by her acting abilities. He was also disquieted by them. Fooling Vanderloord was one thing. How was Harry supposed to know what was real and what wasn't?

The men finished the coffee and sandwiches and the meeting began to wind down.

"So you want to work as a foreign services officer. Where did you go to university?" Vanderloord asked Lies.

"McGill. I majored in political science," she replied promptly, which Harry suspected wasn't true. She'd been evasive about her background from the start, even with him, no doubt so she could change it to suit her purposes whenever necessary.

Like now.

"I studied political science and international law at McGill, although it would have been well before your time," Vanderloord said.

That was why she'd said McGill. She already knew Vanderloord had attended the Canadian institution. She really was good at her job.

"I didn't know you studied law," Harry said to the other man.

"I've never practiced. I got involved in a business opportunity straight out of university and here I am." Vanderloord shrugged. "The rest is history."

Lies's face was alive with eager interest. "What kind of

business opportunity? How did you know it was the right career path to take? Weren't you at all sorry to give up on your education? I mean, you must have intended to practice law when you took it."

Her excitement and enthusiasm were exactly the right level for someone young and ambitious and in search of a mentor, and Vanderloord wasn't any more immune to it than Harry would have been if he'd been in his shoes. His responding smile was warm and lingered on her in a way that had Harry tightening an imaginary fist.

"A degree only starts you out on a life path. You have no idea where that path will eventually lead. A friend came to me with an idea for exporting goods. He knew my family had connections in shipbuilding in the Netherlands. We spoke to a few other friends whose families also had foreign connections. Things progressed from there." Vanderloord stood. He addressed Harry. "I should be going. I know you're busy and I have another meeting in twenty minutes. It will take me that long to make my way through traffic." He reached across the desk to shake Harry's hand. "Thank you for your time. It was very generous of you on such short notice."

Lies jumped to her feet, the skirt of her dress swirling around her thighs. She practically glowed with adulation. "I'll walk you out."

She returned ten minutes later, just as Harry began to worry that she was taking too long and wonder what she and Vanderloord might be talking about.

"He invited me to a wine bar Sunday evening so I can tell him how Tiësto was," Lies announced, looking pleased.

Harry was not. "You're going to a rave by yourself?"

"No. I'm taking my cousin Yasmin, the one who lives in Haarlem. I would have thought you'd be more interested that I'm meeting Bernard Sunday night," she added.

He'd thought so too. But his worry had shifted. "You'll be safe enough in public with him. I'm more concerned about two young women going to a concert alone."

"I asked you to go with me and you said no. You weren't concerned then," she pointed out. "I believe your exact words were, 'Not even at gunpoint.'"

"Because I didn't think you were serious about going at all, let alone by yourself."

"I'm not going by myself. I'm taking Yasmin."

They were talking in circles and it was getting them nowhere. He had to leave for the airport where he was meeting up with a trade mission of contractors and government officials arriving from Canada, here to check out shipbuilding operations.

Harry considered his options and chose the one he could live with. "I'll pick you up after the concert and see that you both get home safely."

"I'm not turning down a free ride, so thank you."

Her quick capitulation raised his suspicions. He'd been preparing for an argument. Why hadn't he gotten one?

"What time does the show end?"

"It starts around eight o'clock, so my best guess is 2 a.m."

Now it made sense. She was teasing because she thought it was too late for him, but the six-hour time difference meant the Canadian trade mission delegates he was hosting would take the weekend to adjust to the change and get some sightseeing in. They'd be out drinking until well after midnight on a Saturday night, and having to drive her home later on gave him an excellent excuse to stay sober.

"I can forgo my nine o'clock bedtime this once." He

adjusted the cuffs of his shirt so they aligned properly with the sleeves of his suit. "I'm sorry the lunch meeting with Vanderloord wasn't more productive."

"Nice try," Lies replied. "I've told you where he and I are going to meet. That was our agreement. What I learn from him is off limits."

He'd agreed to nothing, which unfortunately made no difference. She didn't answer to him. He hated this.

Hated it.

The plane with the Canadian delegates was due to land in thirty minutes. They'd need time to clear customs, but he also had to find parking. He edged his chair aside with his shin and came around the corner of his desk. Lies stood between him and the closed office door.

She'd been so frustratingly unfazed by what had happened between them in the car the other night, when he'd lost his head. She'd accepted his apology and even shouldered a portion of the blame. He'd thought she was inexperienced, but that could well have been part of an act. Did nothing bother her?

How was a man supposed to know where he stood?

There would be no honesty stage in a relationship with her. There'd be no trust either. He'd lose his mind worrying not only about her safety, but who she was with and what they were doing, and this wasn't like him. He'd never been jealous or possessive before. No woman had ever confused him as much as she did. Even now, knowing better and despite where they were standing, he longed to back her up against the wall and slide his hands under the short skirt of that dress.

Her blue eyes were on his face, reading his thoughts far better than he could read hers.

He reached past her for the door handle. "Text me after

the concert tomorrow night when you're ready for me to pick you up. I'm looking forward to meeting your cousin."

He was curious to see how Lies behaved when she was with family.

To see who she really was.

CHAPTER SEVEN

HARRY WAS AS GOOD as his word.

Lies texted him a half hour before the concert ended to give him a head's up, as well as the option to change his mind if he wanted. He'd sent her a reply that he was already waiting for them on a street that bordered the town square where the venue was being held.

When she and Yasmin finally tumbled outside with the dispersing crowd, he was already parked beneath a streetlight where he couldn't be missed. The bored expression he wore as he scanned the throng surging toward him said he was out of his element and unbothered by it. Boredom changed to alertness when he singled her out, separating her from the masses in a way that snatched the air from her lungs. She waved to acknowledge she'd seen him too.

Yasmin pulled up short when she spotted Harry's black luxury sedan. A side-eyed lift of one brow said she wasn't impressed.

"What kind of personal assistant job gives you a high-end flat and a boss who drives you around at three o'clock in the morning in a car such as that? Would your parents approve?"

Lies, her sense of humor enhanced with the help of a few drinks, found it hilarious that she was being chastised by a younger cousin with worse taste in men than her own. She pressed a forefinger against her upper lip in a wasted attempt to stave off a fit of giggles. "I told you. The flat was vacant and since I'm only here for a few months, the embassy said I could use it. And as for the type of boss Harry is..." This hyperawareness of him was private, not something she wished to discuss. She wasn't about to bring it to Yasmin's attention. "Once you meet him you'll see how ridiculous you sound."

He got out of the car to greet them.

"I take it you had a good time," he said.

Lies pulled herself together and made the introductions. "Harry, this is my cousin Yasmin. Yasmin, Harry. My boss."

In her boots Yasmin stood half a head above Harry, but he didn't seem to find it at all awkward—another point in his favor. "The resemblance is uncanny," he said, glancing between the two women. "Except for the color of your hair, you could be twins."

"Thank you. Everyone says so," Yasmin replied. "I'm glad they do. I think Lies is beautiful."

"She is." Harry's gaze lingered on Lies, making her skin prickle as if he'd actually touched her. "You both are," he added as he opened the back door of the car for Yasmin, then ushered Lies into the front passenger seat.

Lies wasn't modest, and there was a definite family resemblance, but in her opinion Yasmin, with her dark hair and extra height, was the truly beautiful one. She wore a midriff-baring white halter top and matching mini skirt paired with thigh-length, high-heeled red boots, whereas Lies had dressed for comfort. She'd chosen a sleeveless black tank, low rider jeans, and slouchy, flat-heeled black suede leather boots.

"How was the concert?" Harry asked as the oversized car crawled through narrow streets packed solid with people.

Yasmin beamed at him in the rearview mirror. "Wonderful. Very noisy. There were three members of the royal family and a few Ajax players in the VIP section with us."

Ajax was a Dutch professional soccer team and its players were superstars in the Netherlands. One had gotten Yasmin's phone number from her. Another had asked Lies for hers as well but she'd politely refused to give it to him. She wasn't interested in spoiled athletes— although a year ago, if he'd asked for her name first, she might have been tempted.

Yasmin, gregarious, liked to speak English whenever given the chance. It wasn't long before she'd teased a smile out of Harry. The two of them carried the conversation during the short trip to Lies's flat.

"What was Lies like as a little girl?" Harry asked.

"Fearless," Yasmin said promptly. "Determined. Quiet. If there was trouble she was usually in the middle of it. She's still the same."

"I'm not sure I believe the quiet part," Harry replied. "She has strong opinions and she doesn't mind sharing them."

He was supposed to be her employer so Lies stayed in character and didn't contradict him. Her cousin, however, was fair game. "All of those things could be said about you too, Yasmin," she pointed out. "Except for being quiet."

Yasmin nodded cheerfully in the back seat. "It's true. They could."

Harry asked her if she'd ever been to Canada and when she said yes, what she'd enjoyed most about it.

"Really? Niagara Falls?" His incredulity had both women laughing. "Did Lies send you over it in a barrel?"

"You know her very well," Yasmin congratulated him. "Although she'd have tried it out first to see if it could be done."

Again, Harry's eyes were on Lies. "I don't know her at all."

Fingers of regret tickled some of the joy out of the evening. He'd never believe she was as much herself when she was alone with him as she was with Yasmin—which might well be for the best.

The two women got out of the car at Lies's flat.

Before closing the door, Lies rested her hand on the frame and leaned inside to say a final goodnight. "Thank you. It was very thoughtful of you to see us home."

"Don't worry. I'll think of some way for you to pay me back."

She had to press her tongue to the roof of her mouth to hold back the multitude of smartass suggestions she longed to make. If they'd been alone she wouldn't have shown any restraint.

They were barely through the building's main door before Yasmin spoke up. "Why didn't you tell me your boss has a crush on you?"

The idea of Harry having something as childish as a crush on a woman was too ridiculous for words. "Because I don't make up stories," Lies replied. So much for not wanting to discuss it. Yasmin would never let it go now. They climbed a narrow flight of stairs as they talked. "And he's not a twelve-year-old boy."

"He likes you," Yasmin insisted. "He's also very attractive—at least he is when he stops being so serious. So why haven't you done anything about it?"

"Like" might be too strong a word for how Harry felt about her. She unlocked the door to her flat and flicked a switch. Light flooded the small entry. "He isn't my type."

Yasmin tugged off her tall boots with a groan of relief. "You mean because you'd never have to worry about him being involved in organized crime?"

"Because he can be a little too..." Lies refused to say boring. Whatever Harry was, he wasn't that.

"Mature?" Yasmin's boots dropped from her hands and she kicked them aside. "Responsible? Intelligent?" She flopped on the sofa and propped her bare feet on the coffee table, crossing her ankles. "Be honest, Lies. You've always dated men you know won't interfere with your freedom. They've passed in and out of your life. You like parts of them but not everything about them. There's nothing not to like about Harry. And no. You wouldn't have to worry about him being involved in organized crime." She studied Lies. "I'm not certain he could have the same confidence in you."

Lies let those words settle in. "You think *I'm* involved in criminal activity?"

Yasmin scrunched up her nose. "I think you like taking too many risks and you keep too many secrets. You never talk about your work."

Was that why Yasmin had introduced her to her friend Baart—not because Yasmin respected her opinion, but because she believed Lies would be able to recognize a fellow criminal?

Lies had then proved her right by being able to do so. Another fit of giggles overcame her. Poor Yasmin. She was as worried about Lies as Lies had been about her.

"I work for a Canadian embassy," she reminded her

cousin, once she could speak. "My job involves discretion. That's why I don't talk much about it. We're also trained to watch for criminal behavior in the people wanting to immigrate to or do business with Canada." All of which was close enough to the truth to be credible.

Relief spilled from Yasmin's eyes. "If that's true, then you do need to have more care with the men you date. They could ruin your career. An even better reason why you should give Harry a chance," she persisted. "He's different. And you could talk about your work with him."

No she couldn't, and he'd hate that. He valued honesty and her work was all about deception. "You met him for fifteen minutes. How could you possibly know that for certain?"

"Is he different?" Yasmin demanded.

"Well, yes. That doesn't mean he's better than other men I've known." If anything he was far more complicated than most. She tried to turn the conversation around. "Would you date him?"

"Not right now." Yasmin yawned and stretched her arms over her head. "I have a striker from Ajax lined up. I'm not ready for someone like Harry. But if I were a few years older, then yes, I would. Harry is the type of man a smart woman marries. You should grab him before someone else does."

"You make me sound like an old woman. I'm not ready for marriage."

"No? You turned down a chance to go out with an Ajax goalkeeper."

"Because he didn't even ask for my name."

"You wouldn't care about his name either if you were only interested in fun. Therefore, you're ready for something more serious. You know I'm right." Yasmin yawned again. "I'm going to bed. Don't wake me until it's time for my train."

Lies sat at the bistro table by the sliding windows, her chin cupped in her hand, and watched the sleeping neighborhood as she waited for Yasmin to finish in the bathroom they shared. She was only three years older than her cousin. She had an exciting career that left her little time for relationships. Marriage was the furthest thing from her mind.

And there was no need to wonder how Harry would react to Yasmin's suggestion that she pursue him. He'd remind her that Plan A was in effect.

She stilled. Was that why he'd been so personable in the car and asked questions about her as a little girl? Had he been trying to see if he could fool Yasmin into believing he was interested in her? Was he trying his hand at deception too?

She discarded the possibility. He wasn't that good an actor. Harry really was aware of her, at least on a physical level. And she was equally aware of him. She could hardly deny it when she could still feel his touch on her skin. But neither could she deny that they weren't right for each other. Lies would need to be trusted by any man she became seriously involved with and he'd never trust her. He'd been jaded by his experience with Alcine.

Never mind that he hadn't loved her.

Lies had searched through the embassy's files until she'd located publicity photos of Harry and Alcine together. She'd told herself she'd wanted to find out the type of woman Bernard found attractive.

She'd also been curious as to Harry's taste.

Alcine was tall, elegant in style, with an olive complexion. She had long, straight dark hair. In some photos she'd worn it upswept, in others loose. She appeared to prefer classic clothing that showed off a model-thin figure and obviously knew how to play up her best features.

Something about her body language, however, had expressed discontentment to Lies. In the photos of her posing with Harry she'd had her face turned away from him and there was a subtle physical distance. To Lies they looked more like business partners than lovers. From what little Harry had told her, their private relationship had been no different.

On a whim she'd also searched for the Albanian diplomat's wife—the twenty-three-year-old former model. She had long, curly black hair, very fair skin, and decidedly trashy, although expensive, taste in clothing. Her gowns were cut far too low to be appropriate for anything but a Hollywood awards ceremony. They did, however, illustrate her plastic surgeon's genius for breast enhancement.

The only common denominators between the two women Lies had found were the ones she'd expected— both were unhappy in their relationships, ambitious, and had access to information a third party such as Bernard might find useful.

That Bernard had already been romantically involved with Harry's former girlfriend made Lies's own position precarious. Harry had made it no secret that he didn't like Bernard. If Bernard liked to play games, however, then going after a second woman Harry had expressed an interest in—one who could also get him any information he wanted—might prove an irresistible challenge.

She was counting on it.

She heard the bathroom door open, then the spare bedroom door close. She rose from the table. Tomorrow evening she would have to sit down with Bernard Vanderloord and pretend to be infatuated.

She could well imagine Harry's opinion on that.

Lies saw Yasmin off at the train station before bicycling to the wine bar where she was to meet Bernard. She planned to establish her alibi with him—that she was indeed a spoiled embassy junior staffer, nothing more. The game required patience.

The evening was warm for late September and the streets were crowded with people taking advantage of the fair weather. She locked her bicycle in a stand outside of the bar.

Inside, Bernard was seated at a corner booth with a drink in front of him. She noted they'd have to sit next to each other on the L-shaped bench and doubted if the intimate arrangement was accidental.

Perfect.

So why did she feel so uneasy about it?

"You look very lovely tonight," Bernard said, rising to greet her. "As usual." He gave her the friendly Dutch greeting of three quick kisses on either cheek and waited for her to be seated, then reclaimed his own before ordering her a glass of red wine. "How was the concert?"

"Excellent. I was assured that my hearing should return by Tuesday."

"I'm sorry I missed it."

He sounded so far from sorry that Lies had to laugh, then challenge him on it. "You are not."

"No," he admitted. "But you can tell me all about it."

"That's very selfless of you. I'm sure it qualifies you for some kind of award."

She told him about the concert while she sipped the wine, which was very good. When she said so, he ordered a bottle over her protests. It was hardly a new ploy. He'd drink very little of it while topping off her glass at every opportunity. It was his motive for this meeting she was uncertain of. He liked younger women. But did he like them more than information?

"How did you come to be working with the embassy?" he asked. "I know you have a background in political science and are interested in the foreign services, and you speak the languages here, but most people have some sort of connection for diplomatic positions."

"My father is a Dutch diplomat," Lies said. "In his earlier years he spent a lot of time in Indonesia. That's where he met my mother, who's Canadian. She's why he now works in Ottawa." All of which would be verified if he chose to do a search. Using her name or the keywords she'd given him would raise red flags in the government databases. Harry's name too, along with his profile information, had been flagged. "He got me an interview, but I like to think I earned this position on my own."

Bernard was watching her closely. "What's your relationship with Harry?"

"He's my boss."

"He seems very interested in you."

Lies looked at him over the rim of her glass as she took a measured sip of the wine. She enjoyed this. Establishing a cover story was like arranging the men on a chessboard. Each move was a gambit. Bernard's questions were open-ended, inviting her to confide in him, but still, she was getting no sense of what he really wanted from her. For her part, she was trying to give the impression that her interest in Harry was based solely around what he could do for her career. She also wanted him to believe that she liked to take risks.

The latter wasn't at all a stretch of her acting abilities.

She didn't set the glass down but continued to hold it, rolling the stem between her fingers, so he couldn't top it up until she was ready. She smiled as if sharing a secret. "I make him nervous. He's afraid I'll offend someone important because he thinks I ask too many questions."

"It must be uncomfortable—to be watched so closely every day."

She shrugged. "Harry is Harry. He's good to work for and he's generous about introducing me to people, even if he does tend to hover. I don't like updating his electronic filing system though." She made a face as she tossed out the lure. "He might as well have taken a bunch of papers and thrown them in a basket. I've been sorting unlabeled data for weeks. I have no idea what's important and what's not."

She'd just let him know she had free access to embassy defense information and very little discretion. The next move was his.

"Will you be going to the helicopter expo with him?"

The helicopter expo was an annual international event hosted by the Dutch government and tended to draw the same crowd every year. He'd hardly need Harry's connections for that. She'd thought he would ask about the Canadian trade mission here for the shipbuilding tours that Harry was hosting.

"Of course." The expo was on Harry's agenda because of the visiting trade commission. Helicopters were used on ships all the time. Planning for landing capabilities at sea would be part of a shipbuilding contract.

"If you're serious about advancing your career, I have a few people I can introduce you to. I'd be honored if you'd accompany me to dinner on opening night."

She felt his hand on her thigh beneath the table, very briefly. He was testing her to see how she'd respond.

She set her glass down and allowed him to refill it, then met his gaze. "I'd love to. Thank you. You're very kind to offer."

After that, the conversation switched to non-work-related topics. Bernard might be tight-lipped about his business, but when it came to his personal life he was far more forthcoming. It was easy for Lies to see how he'd attracted the Albanian diplomat's young wife. Bernard lived a high lifestyle. He owned a sailboat he took out almost every weekend in the summer. He'd white-water-rafted in the Amazon and climbed Kilimanjaro. He'd gone on safari in South Africa several times.

Other than the sailing, however, he talked very little about his travels within Europe. To Lies, it was a telling omission. She also knew from her research that, despite being Canadian by birth, he steered clear of North American travel completely—at least under his own name. It wasn't as difficult as it should be for people with the right connections to maintain a number of fake passports. It would never be one hundred percent impossible.

She enjoyed the rest of the evening. Bernard was an entertaining companion. When she turned down more wine, reminding him she had to bicycle home—it was illegal in the Netherlands to ride a bicycle while intoxicated, a law strictly enforced and she was an embassy employee—he didn't persist but finished the bottle himself.

After the better part of two hours had passed, she

mentioned how late it was and that she had to work in the morning. He offered to see her home, but he'd had more to drink than she did and his flat was within walking distance, so she declined. Never once, however, did she get the sense he was not in control.

They parted ways at a street corner. Bernard leaned in as if to kiss her, only to offer the same three perfectly respectable brushes of the cheek they'd shared earlier. It was silly of her to feel so relieved. A kiss was nothing.

And yet she suspected Harry would disagree. The way he'd kissed her had definitely not been nothing.

She cycled the long route that led along one of the canals ringing the heart of the old city, taking the extra time to clear her head. She'd learned nothing worth reporting to John at CSIS headquarters in Ottawa, and yet she believed she'd made significant inroads. Bernard would never trust her because he trusted no one, but he could be made to underestimate her.

Harry was waiting outside of her flat when she finally arrived home. He shouldn't be here. If he were seen it might be perceived as prearranged.

Her heart leaped at the sight of him all the same.

He was an attractive man, dignified and well-dressed, who gave off an aura of quiet but confident authority. The lightweight cotton navy sweater, the relaxed-fit designer jeans, and red chukka boots showed another side to his character and it suited him perfectly—expensive, without being either dated or trendy.

His dark eyes were always so serious. One had to look closely to discern the tightly-leashed heat in them. Fire scorched over her as his gaze touched her. Bernard's hand had been on her thigh and yet she'd felt nothing. Certainly not the breathless excitement and confusion Harry caused in her with a mere brush of his eyes. If Bernard's expectations were raised through a little harmless flirtation, it was all part of the game.

Harry's expectations, however...

She should be more careful. Their flirtations were hardly harmless. This wasn't the same as the situation with Michael, but she wasn't convinced her bosses would fully appreciate the difference.

"You shouldn't be here," she said.

"And you should have been home hours ago. I called several times."

He sounded like an over-possessive and jealous boyfriend, something she would never have tolerated in any other man, but Harry was playing his part far better than she'd given him credit for. Plus he'd expressed—more than once—a genuine concern for her safety, and for that, she'd give him a pass.

He held her bicycle while she unlocked the door to the storage garage, then wheeled it inside behind her and tucked it into an empty space on one of the racks. She locked the tire before pocketing the key.

As she straightened, she and Harry collided. He'd deliberately moved closer so that contact between them would be unavoidable. Her fingers clutched at his sleeve to steady herself. They stared at each other. She held her breath.

"Can I come up?" he finally asked when the long stretch of silence made it obvious she wasn't going to extend any invitation.

She slowly exhaled. They both knew what invariably happened whenever they were alone together. Her conscience nudged her, giving one final warning. Her bosses would never approve.

What they don't know won't hurt them, the daredevil inside her whispered back. It wasn't as if Harry would kiss and tell. He didn't have it in him to be anything other than discreet.

She settled for a compromise. "On the understanding that we aren't going to talk about my evening," she warned him. "Or about work at all." If she allowed him to come to her flat, he didn't get to accuse her of playing games with him. What happened next would be straightforward.

This was about sex, plain and simple.

His face clouded over. He was going to walk away rather than argue the point. His expression said so. Part of her was relieved. Another, bigger, part wasn't.

Before disappointment could fully manifest however, he acquiesced. "Fine."

He held his palm pressed to the small of her back on the short ride in the lift. His thumb rubbed back and forth over her hip in a discreet but effective gesture that left her uncertain of her legs' abilities to keep her upright. She couldn't look at him, whereas he never took his eyes from her face. She felt them on her as plainly as she felt the weight of his hand.

They were barely inside the door of her flat before he had her pressed against the wall.

CHAPTER EIGHT

WHAT HE WAS DOING was insanity.

It was also so out of character he could hardly believe it of himself. But Harry had wanted Lies from the moment he'd first laid eyes on her in John Carmichael's office and he planned to have her. He needed to get her out of his system. Out of his head.

She wore tight leggings and a loose, sleeveless tunic over a T-shirt. He lifted the hem of the tunic and tugged it over her head, dropping it to the floor. He took her hips in his hands and her lips with his mouth. Her height meant their pelvises touched, his erection hard on her belly, and he would have loved to take her right there.

He had to slow things down. This wasn't going to happen at the door of her flat where anyone happening by could hear them. It was going to be loud and he'd be taking his time. He wasn't the only one who'd find satisfaction tonight.

Continuing to kiss her, he hooked his thumbs over the waistband of her leggings and touched naked flesh. She gasped against his lips, arching her back, the feel of the soft mounds of her breasts on his chest impeded by the sweater he wore. Her fingers went to his belt. She unbuckled it, sliding it slowly from the loops of his jeans. It clattered to the tiled floor. Her teeth grazed his lower lip. She drew it into her mouth, the tip of her tongue playing with it. He had his hands inside her leggings, cupping her buttocks, his palms under the thin scrap of her panties, when a problem presented itself. He hadn't used protection in years.

"I'm clean," he said. He'd had himself checked after he found out about Alcine's affair. "Do I need a condom?"

"So am I. And no. I'm on the pill."

"Bedroom," he commanded. "Now."

She twisted in his arms, catching the buttoned front of his jeans with her fingers as she kicked off her shoes. "This way."

She led him down the narrow hall and past the darkened living room where city lights sparkled through the sheer curtains she'd left drawn closed. Her bedroom was small, barely large enough for the queen-sized bed, but right now the bed was all that mattered to him. Soft light from the street spilled into the dimly-lit room. The far wall, facing the building next door, was crafted entirely of heavy, opaque glass panels. Clothing littered the floor and draped off the top of the open closet door. Tidy, she was not. He noticed it all in passing. His primary focus remained on Lies and how beautiful she looked, all lithe-bodied and tousled blond curls.

She peeled off her T-shirt, revealing delectable breasts encased in a plain white, serviceable bra. The leggings followed. Beneath them were plain white cotton bikinis. His hard-on, straining against the fly of his jeans, throbbed with an even greater insistence. She had not an ounce of self-consciousness, which he hadn't expected of her anyway, but the lack of frilly, feminine lingerie loosened the tight knot in his chest that had tortured him all evening at the thought of her in bed with another man. Lies might be far different from most women he knew, but in his experience, this wasn't what one wore if she were planning a seduction. She'd said there was a limit to how far she'd go to gather information and the evidence indicated she meant it.

She sat on the edge of the bed, leaning back on her hands with her long, naked legs dangling over the side, and watched him undress. Shoes first, then the sweater. When he began to unbutton his jeans she reached out to intervene, catching the backs of his thighs with her heels and pulling him closer to the bed. She worked the zipper, easing its throat carefully down the teeth, then slipped her fingers inside the open fly to close around his length as he sprang free. He hissed a breath through clenched teeth. He shucked out of his jeans and his briefs and kicked them aside. He was totally naked and she had him in her hand, and God, she was so incredibly beautiful as she ran her fist up and down him and teased the backs of his legs with her bare toes.

She would have taken him in her mouth if he hadn't stopped her, not that he wanted to, but because he intended for her to enjoy this as much as he did and the night would be over too soon if she did. He was in no hurry. When it came to getting Lies out of his system, he'd do it right.

He pressed her flat on the bed. Then, he flipped her onto her belly. She still had on her plain panties and bra, which he found oddly exciting, although she wouldn't be wearing them long. He dipped his fingers beneath the fabric and into her damp heat, first one, then a second, in and out. She moaned encouragement, but not nearly loud enough. The hell with not being overheard. He planned to wake up the neighbors.

"Do you like that?" he asked, removing his fingers. "Do you want more of it?"

"Yes." She lifted her hips, parting her thighs as she did so. "*Yes*. Don't stop now. I'm so close."

He had to shut his eyes to help him concentrate, to keep from easing his erection inside her instead, because it was still too soon for that. Ego now factored in. There'd be more than one orgasm in this for her. She was going to remember him and their night together. She was going to dream about it at the office while she sat at her desk, thinking up new ways to torment him. The joke was on her. He knew his way around women. He explored her folds with the tip of his finger. She was wet, she was hot, and right now she was *his*.

When he found the tiny nub, she cried out his name and an admonishment—half of pleasure, half in frustration. "Harry! Stop *teasing* me. Who knew you were cruel?"

He took that as a challenge. She brought out the worst in him. Soon she was panting, grinding against the palm of his hand as he worked his fingers deep inside her, trying his damnedest not to come all over them both. She cried out, her back stiffening, her tight inner muscles clenching. When she collapsed, her whole body trembled. "Oh my *God* that was amazing."

Pride had him smiling with satisfaction. But she'd been torturing him for weeks and it was payback time. "We aren't finished yet."

He eased the panties down her legs with one hand, slowly, while he stroked her cleft with the other. Once the panties were gone, he knelt over her and rubbed the length of his erection between the cheeks of her buttocks. He slid his palms up the length of her narrow back, panting at the sensation of all that smooth, naked skin. His fingers snagged in the clasp of her bra and he unfastened it with ease. He began again, at the base of her spine, trailing the tip of his tongue to the base of her neck. He nipped at the tender side of her throat, then gently sucked, careful not to leave any marks. He eased his hands beneath her and cupped her breasts in his palms. They were swollen, the tips peaked and firm, and he wanted desperately to taste them again as he had that night in the car. He nudged her hip with his knee, and taking the cue, she wriggled onto her back.

He took a moment to admire what he'd done to her. There was enough light in the room for him to see how flushed her cheeks were, and the heat in those languorous, heavy-lidded eyes. She wasn't delicate or fussy, which only added to the potentials for pleasure, and he'd barely begun. He discarded the bra, untangling it from her arms.

He took her breasts in his hands, feeling their weight, kissing the tip of first one, then the other. He suckled the nipple, tormenting it with his tongue. She bucked on the bed beneath him. Reaching between his legs, she stroked his erection.

That was all he allowed her to do. This was going to be faster than he'd wanted because he couldn't wait any longer. His balls were so heavy they hurt.

Planting his hands on either side of her head, he leaned down to kiss her. The tips of her fingers bit into his thighs as her tongue thrust against his. She hooked her legs around his waist.

He positioned himself at her opening, and with a distinct lack of finesse and control, thrust inside her. Her legs tightened, her whole body arching as she took his entire length. She threw her head back, her eyes closed, moaning with pleasure. "Harder, Harry. *Faster*."

"I'm going to come." His breathing was ragged and he

was about to explode. He could feel it building. He thrust harder and faster, just as she'd asked for, with no rhythm or thought other than to make her come again with him. Her head touched the headboard with each jerk of his hips.

"Now, Harry. *Now!*"

Her fingers scrabbled at the cheeks of his ass. She sank her teeth into his shoulder, not hard, just a nip, but enough to add to the excitement shooting from his groin to his ribcage. He felt the first ripples of her orgasm massaging his shaft and was lost.

"Son of a *bitch*," he growled, giving up on restraint. He came on an explosion of light that burned into the backs of his eyelids, blinding him for a few moments. When his vision cleared Lies was exhausted and shaking beneath him, the aftershocks of her orgasm wringing the last of his out of him.

He rolled off her, stretching out on the bed, waiting for his heart to quit pounding so he could breathe normally again. He'd foreseen the excitement of making love to her. It was the intensity of her enthusiasm that had been so…unexpected.

The hammering of his heart had progressed to his ears. Then he realized it wasn't his heart at all.

The neighbors in the next flat were banging on the bedroom wall behind his head.

Harry left in the wee hours of the morning, while she was asleep, no doubt driven by second thoughts and a guilty conscience.

He'd have to deal with his conscience on his own. Lies

had problems to work through too. She rinsed soap from her body with the hand-held sprayer linked by a flexible hose to the tiled shower wall of her compact bathroom. Suds swirled around her bare feet, circling the floor drain.

Harry was as good in bed as she'd suspected he'd be. He'd been all about seeing to her satisfaction. Every inch of her skin hummed with contentment. But he was in danger of becoming a competent lover. He was too much in control of his own pleasure, keeping it carefully contained until certain of hers. Whatever his and Alcine's relationship had been in bed, it wasn't adventurous.

That was the other woman's loss. For Lies's part, she'd like to see his natural inclination toward dominance further unleashed so she could figure out his preferences too. Given a bit of encouragement, she'd bet he'd be naughty. Harry in bed was not at all the same man he was at the office.

Speaking of which, she was about to be late. She turned off the water, which had grown cold, and scooped a towel from the shelf next to the shower enclosure. As she dried off, she tried to decide what her next step should be. While she had no regrets over last night, did she tell the CSIS director that she'd slept with Canada's aerospace and defense trade commissioner while on assignment? Or did she keep to herself the fact that she'd slept with a man she admired very much?

Pretending to be involved with each other was one thing. They'd gone a step further, and if she had her way, they'd go further still. While sleeping with Harry wasn't illegal, immoral, or even unethical—what she did on her own time was still her own business—Harry had brought Bernard to the attention of CSIS. He'd made no secret of the fact he didn't care for him. There was personal history between the two men. Not to mention that she'd been warned to keep her integrity intact because there was a lot riding on this investigation—CSIS was after the Canadian Minister of Defence, and except at the discretion of the director, CSIS reported to him. Any kink in that slender chain could cause problems for John Carmichael. Harry's integrity—and motives—might well be called into question too. Ugly things could happen behind closed office doors.

Lies would have to be very careful that any information leading to the minister she collected from Bernard was ironclad and verifiable. She'd keep last night off the record and do her best to make sure what she and Harry did when they were alone didn't attract any interest, because there was going to be a repeat of last night.

He could count on it.

She didn't kid herself into thinking there'd be a happily ever after. They lived far different lives and bottom line, he hated hers. They'd both just come out of bad relationships and neither one of them was ready to try again. They were in this for the sex. The really great sex.

That was it.

With that goal firmly established she finished dressing, grabbed some bread and cheese from the kitchen, then retrieved her bicycle from the garage. She arrived at work with seconds to spare.

Harry was already in his office, doing an unruffled impersonation of a permanent fixture. Anyone could be excused for thinking he lived here. He had papers strewn across his desk and was sipping a coffee.

He lifted his head as she entered his field of vision on the way to her desk. "Lies, can I speak with you for a moment?"

He couldn't possibly be planning to tell her last night had been a mistake. Not already and not here at the office.

"Nothing good ever comes from a conversation that starts off with those words," she replied, although she stopped and backed up a few steps.

The fine lines bracketing his firm mouth deepened for a breath, then smoothed into faint humor. She had a moment's vivid recollection of the tug of his mouth on her breast, and his tongue tracking the length of her belly, and her stomach did a tight, eager dance. She had a burning desire to shake all of that office decorum. If not for the lack of curtains at the windows, she'd bet she could talk him into having sex on his desk. Of course there was always after hours with the lights out to consider.

And she'd have to convince him that it was all his idea.

"I'll rephrase that," he said, dispelling her fantasy. "I need your help with the trade delegates at the helicopter expo in Amsterdam tomorrow. I've lined up meetings for them and you'll monitor their schedules to keep them on track. Add your name to the registration list."

She'd completely forgotten to tell Harry that Bernard expected her to be at that expo too. She might have to relax her rule about no work-talk in bed in the other rooms of her flat. If they couldn't talk shop at the office, in public, or the bedroom, their information-exchange options became too limited and they risked more of these snafus.

"I was invited to dinner tomorrow night at the venue's restaurant," she said.

He set the coffee cup down and tugged at the sleeve of his suit, a sure sign he was annoyed and not wanting to let on. A motorcycle backfired somewhere in morning traffic outside of the embassy. "I assume your host will be picking up the tab."

Harry wasn't a spendthrift by any means, but neither did he worry about the nickels and dimes of his department's business expenditures, meaning yes, he was ticked. Since she wasn't his personal assistant in real life, that was his problem not hers. And she couldn't really say she cared for his tone. Even though they weren't in a committed relationship, she slept with one man at a time. She wasn't Alcine.

Despite all evidence to the contrary, however, Harry was human. He'd been hurt and had issues with trust. She of all people could sympathize.

"Is there a government policy against a staff member having dinner with an embassy client at a public function that I wasn't made aware of?" she asked.

Dark brown eyes studied her. She could see the wheels spinning, then the wariness settling in. "Why do you ask?"

"I wouldn't want to give the impression it was anything but business. If it were personal, we'd go to my flat."

The frown pinching his eyebrows together relaxed its tight grip. "There's no such policy. The restaurant is a good place to network and shouldn't interfere with embassy business," he conceded. "Just make sure the delegates show up for their meetings in the right places at the right times."

Harry had handed her an excellent opportunity to find out what connections the delegates made while they were here, because gathering intelligence was like assembling a puzzle. One never knew where the pieces might fit.

"I'll register this morning," she promised.

That was the last chance they had to speak for the remainder of the day. She wouldn't be seeing him that evening. He was taking the trade delegation for a dinner meeting with local shipping contractors. She'd love to sit in on those meetings, but it really would look odd for his personal assistant to be with him. The Dutch contractors would see it as pretentious and Harry had to work with them.

The evening was long and boring without Harry to distract her, so she worked on some notes for her case file. She also had a few pieces of equipment that required reassembling. She'd taken them apart to get them through customs when she'd entered the country. After that, she went to bed. She was normally a night owl but between the concert on the weekend and the late night with Harry, her internal clock had taken a beating.

She fell asleep in a jumble of sheets that smelled of Harry's aftershave and a night of fantastic sex, disappointed that she was alone and he hadn't called.

She awoke with enough time to take an unhurried shower before catching the train headed for Schiphol. The trade expo was fifteen minutes from the international airport. The day was wet and cold so she carried her umbrella. Underneath her raincoat she wore a cream-colored cotton knit turtleneck sweater and black dress pants. Her practical shoes were the ones she wore to her office in Ottawa. They were the most comfortable pair she owned and she'd be on her feet the whole day.

From the metro station she found the bus that traveled to the venue. The registration desk was overwhelmed. Three British attendees, who'd obviously just gotten off a flight, were experiencing frustration, so Lies stepped in to help them out.

Once registered herself, with her coat checked and her nametag and pass attached to the lanyard around her neck, she was free. She'd deliberately arrived ahead of Harry and the Canadian delegates because she wanted to wander through the exhibit areas at leisure and chat with exhibitors. Expos were goldmines for gathering intelligence.

It was early afternoon when she spotted Harry and the trade mission delegates near the main entrance. She hurried over to join them and Harry introduced her as his personal assistant, sounding brisk and professional, giving not the slightest hint that he'd had her naked and sobbing his name only two nights before.

And she'd thought he couldn't act.

The fact that he could made her uneasy. She preferred his straightforwardness. It set him apart.

She had the delegates' schedules programmed into her phone. The meetings and seminars were held in a different hall so she led them toward it, pushing her way through the crowd. There were three meetings that interested her, but the one that really caught her attention was between a lawyer representing a Canadian securities company and a Ukrainian helicopter original equipment manufacturer—OEM for short. The helicopter OEM bought parts for repairs from manufacturers operating out of Thailand, India, and Pakistan. Her team leader, Dan, had told her that missing Canadian aircraft parts had been tracked to all three of those countries.

The lawyer's name was Mike Freeland. He was tall, thin, and stooped, with gray, greasy, combed-over hair. The suit he wore cost more than she earned in a month. She placed him in his late forties. His right forefinger and nailbed bore telltale yellow nicotine stains from heavy smoking. His eyes were red-rimmed. He'd either been drinking or visiting a local coffee shop—which, despite its misleading name, was a place to buy soft drugs without fear of arrest.

"Could you grab me a coffee, sweetheart?" he asked her. "I'm too old for the Amsterdam nightlife."

Coffee house it was, then. Lawyers made the worst tourists. They knew exactly what they could get away with and where the line was that couldn't be crossed.

"Of course." She let his condescension roll off her. She was interested in learning more about his connection to the Ukrainian OEM. Political correctness was a small price to pay in exchange. "Black, or cream and sugar?"

"Black."

She brought him his coffee.

Meanwhile, Harry had connected with a Dutch government official and the two were deep in private conversation. She wondered where he'd been last night after his meetings had ended. She felt confident in assuming he hadn't gone to a coffee house with Freeland. He hadn't been at her flat either.

She shook off a niggling of doubt. It was still too soon to worry about where his conscience might be leading him.

Shortly before five o'clock her cellphone rang, displaying Bernard's number.

"You look busy," he said.

He had no idea. It was inconceivable to her how grown men could be so lacking in time management skills. "Where are you?"

"Behind you, three doors to your right."

She was facing the seminar rooms. She turned, spotted him, and waved. "Give me twenty minutes. I'll meet you at the restaurant."

The catering and restaurant area was busy when she arrived. People spilled beyond the ropes sectioning it off from the registration zone. Bernard was near the front of the line, his tall frame and blond head easy enough to pick out.

He was quite impressive Lies conceded, with an air that drew people to him—an especially important personal quality to have in an environment such as this, where business representatives sought out the obvious influencers.

The man he was speaking with looked vaguely familiar. She hung back, trying to place him, and then she had it. She didn't know the second man personally but she'd seen his picture. He was on a CSIS watch list, suspected of domestic terrorism, but had managed to flee Canada before an alert to detain him could be posted. An international helicopter expo wasn't the first place she would have expected to find him and it didn't bode well.

He and Bernard finished their conversation and he walked away. Bernard looked around and spotted her. He raised his hand above the crowd to flag her over. As she approached him she saw the Canadian lawyer, Mike Freeland, a few feet to his left. He and Bernard nodded to each other but they didn't speak.

"Do you know Mr. Freeland?" Lies asked when she reached Bernard's side. The briefcase she carried instead of a purse bumped the person standing next to her and she excused herself to them. Out of habit she automatically checked the outside pocket where she kept her phone to make sure it was secure.

"We went to law school together."

At McGill. Lies felt that rush of excitement which meant she'd stumbled onto a piece of the puzzle and where it might fit. "Is he one of the friends you spoke of who has family connections in other countries?"

"He's hardly a friend. This is the first time I've seen him in years."

That was as evasive a response as she'd ever heard. Something in Bernard's posture said she'd made the right puzzle piece fit. He, a pot-smoking lawyer, and the Canadian Minister of National Defence had all gone to McGill at around the same time. Freeland was in the Netherlands as part of a trade mission and had arranged a last minute meeting with Ukrainians. If that was his background—and it would be easy enough to find out if it was—then she had a worthwhile piece of information to pass on to John Carmichael.

She'd ask Harry a few questions and see what else she could find out about Freeland.

CHAPTER NINE

SHE AND BERNARD ENDED up at a table with three strangers.

Since the event was about networking it was an inconvenience to no one but Lies. The one benefit she got was to see how Bernard interacted with people he didn't know. It turned out he was very charming, despite the obvious fact that the three Germans they'd joined were of no interest to him whatsoever.

It wasn't long before the Germans got up to leave. Within minutes their vacated seats were claimed by Americans.

Partway through her meal, and between the dull, professional chatter, Lies spotted Harry seated four tables over. He was with the Canadian lawyer and another delegate from the trade mission, and a group of people she didn't recognize. The lawyer was deep in conversation with a young, sharp-faced man who looked ill-at-ease in Harry's company. He kept shooting sidelong glances at Harry, who had the intent expression on his face that he used to disguise boredom.

Bernard noticed where her attention continued to stray. "Are you certain you and Harry don't have a personal interest in each other?"

"He's my boss," she reminded him, flustered at having been caught staring. She was normally more circumspect. "That pretty much says it all."

"Ah. I see. It's against Harry's code of ethics."

Without a doubt. If she'd worked for him for real the other night would never have happened. "Never mind that I might have a few ethics myself."

Bernard had the audacity to laugh at her, with genuine humor that stretched to his eyes. "I don't believe you'd allow anything to stand in your way if you were after something you really wanted."

His assessment of her was startling because, while it suited her purposes, it might be a little too close to the truth. Bernard was good at reading people, with a lot of experience behind him, and she'd do well to remember that she was the rookie not him.

They were speaking to each other in Dutch because the conversation was private, but the Americans appeared to be uncomfortable with it so she switched over to English and addressed the entire table. "Women need to be cautious around men if they want to be taken seriously in the business world. Would you gentlemen agree?"

One of the Americans, a bluff, friendly man with red cheeks and a thick Texas accent, shook his head. "It depends on what you mean by cautious. I'd like to think we've come a long way in the last twenty years. The women working for me were hired because they had the right mix of education and experience. They have equal footing."

"Would you have an office affair with one of them? Or condone any relationship between two of your employees if one was in a position of authority over another?" she pressed him. On one hand she wanted Bernard to believe that any interest she had in Harry was all about what he could do for her. And that yes, she would go after whatever she wanted if it would further her career. On the other hand, she was poking the bear. This was a male-dominated industry and the conversations she'd overheard throughout the day reflected that fact.

"That's how I met my first wife," the Texan replied. The others at the table all laughed. He then turned more serious. "I'd be curious as to who was taking advantage of whom. These days nothing's ever so simple. Most women I know would file a sexual harassment suit quick as a wink if a man tried to hold her career over her head. It would be equally possible that she's using him to get a promotion. And that's assuming the man is in the position of power," he added. "My VP of finance is a woman. If she's sleeping with one of her staff, no one's complaining. Her husband might not care for it though. But that's between them."

Lies liked him. She hoped he wasn't all talk.

He also gave her something to think about. She freely acknowledged she might still be defensive over Dan filing that report on her regarding her relationship with Michael. Bernard's words, however, were the ones that continued to ring in her head long after her evening had ended and he was driving her home.

I don't believe you'd allow anything to stand in your way if you were after something you really wanted.

They were an accurate assessment of her. She did go after the things she wanted. It was part of what made her a good intelligence officer. But anyone who danced the fine edge of both sides of the law the way she did faced enormous temptation. She often had to decide between what her conscience could live with, what would benefit the greater good, and which was more important in any given situation.

Sleeping with Harry wasn't only about what she could

live with. For him, she wasn't his employee so that wasn't his issue. It was that he didn't like what she did for a living. He valued trust and he'd never pretended that he trusted her. She'd been wrong to dismiss his struggles with his conscience over sleeping with her as his problem, not hers. It was one they shared equally.

Bernard pulled his car into a vacant parking spot along the side of the wide canal that fronted her flat. Aging alder, willow, and elm trees flourished, their branches drooping over the quiet water. The night was young and he didn't shut off the engine. An elderly woman with a fat pug on a leash waddled past. The pug paused at the flowery shrubs bordering Lies's building, which butted the street, and lifted a hind leg.

"Thank you for dinner and driving me home," Lies said. Bernard had insisted on it when he'd found out she'd used public transit. She'd hoped Harry would offer, but he'd disappeared.

"Aren't you going to invite me in?" Bernard asked.

She was smarter than that. She didn't think he was suspicious of her, but she was hardly going to give him the chance to search through her things if he was. She didn't want him planting a wire in her flat either. That was what she planned on doing to him.

There was also the possibility that Harry might drop in unannounced, and she could well imagine what he'd think if he found Bernard already there.

Which brought up another downside to sleeping with Harry. This constant worrying about what he might think or how he'd react could have a negative impact on her investigation. Maybe Dan was right to be so concerned over who intelligence officers slept with. It wasn't always about giving away secrets. Right now she wasn't paying enough attention to her job.

"My place is a mess," she said, offering it as a shame-faced confession, not the lame excuse that it was. "I'm not set up for entertaining yet. We could go to your place instead." She made the suggestion with youthful enthusiasm, as if it were spur-of-the-moment, when she'd been trying to finagle an invitation to his home all through dinner.

"I'm afraid it isn't convenient for me to have visitors this evening either," Bernard said. "I'm having my condo painted." He was quiet for a moment, as if trying to make up his mind. "I'm having a small dinner party on Saturday. Would you care to join me?"

She gave herself a mental high five. A party with other people in attendance would give her the freedom to move around. It was perfect. "I'd love to."

"I'll pick you up at seven."

He leaned across the console, and before she could prevent it, he kissed her. It was thorough and far from unpleasant. In fact, it was quite nice. He knew what he was doing.

Far better than she did.

The kiss ended. She gathered her briefcase bag and umbrella, scrabbling for the latch on the car door, and nearly knocked over a man on a bicycle in her hurry to get it open. The man swerved to avoid a collision and called angrily over his shoulder for her to watch what she was doing. Lies ignored him, her head a swirl of confusion as she stepped out. Night air tugged at her hair and she reached up to smooth the curls off her cheek.

Bernard, if anything, found her reaction amusing. He rolled down the passenger side window, his smile smug. "I'll call you tomorrow."

She sank onto a bench and watched his car as it crossed the narrow bridge spanning the canal before disappearing into traffic on the far side. The one bright spot was that nothing about her reaction had screamed intelligence officer. There'd been nothing intelligent about it at all.

She rubbed her forehead, closing her eyes as she pulled herself back together. A month ago—maybe even two days—being thoroughly kissed by a man she found attractive wouldn't have bothered her. But now, whether Bernard's kisses were nice or not, he wasn't Harry.

And this.

This wasn't a game she could win.

Harry stared at the ceiling of his bedroom, trying to figure Lies out and where they now stood, or where he wanted them to.

He'd deliberately not stayed the whole night in her bed. If he had it would have led to expectations, more on his part than hers. She was the last thing he needed and he was far from the right man for her. He didn't have the mental fortitude a woman like Lies would require. He'd had a friend who'd lost a finger playing with fireworks when they were kids. Lies was the firecracker and he hated to think of what he stood to lose.

She'd acted as if a man cutting and running after a few hours of great sex was nothing unusual for her, and that was driving him mad, because in his estimation the sex had been better than great. It was all he could do not to head over to her place right now, despite it being well after midnight.

All that stopped him was the fear that any rising expectations might indeed solely be his. Outside of work he should leave her alone. Otherwise he'd never get her out of his head.

His rarely-used landline rang. It perched on the table beside his bed, a few inches out of reach. He fumbled for the light, upsetting the lamp in the process, and gave up on it, answering the phone in the dark. He couldn't read the caller ID, but it could only be one of two people—his mother or Lies—and having either one of them call at this time of night didn't bode well. "Hello?"

"Hi."

It was Lies. She had this number so they could speak in private. While her cellphone might be locked up tighter than Camp David his wasn't, and using a landline was somewhat more secure.

He flopped back on the pillows. He'd left her alone at the expo with Vanderloord. What a stupid move that had been on his part. Worry spiked as to what trouble she'd gotten herself into. "What's wrong?"

"Bernard kissed me."

He couldn't begin to process how he felt about that. Certainly not good, but at least she was safe so he struggled for indifference. He'd known from the beginning how CSIS planned to get information from Vanderloord. He didn't need to hear the details. "Why are you telling me this?"

"Because he kissed *me* and I've been trying to figure out why." Lies's responding impatience to his abruptness did a lot to relax the tightening knot in his gut. "I've been dropping hints for days about how much access to confidential information at the embassy I have and yet he doesn't seem to care. If he's not after information, then what does he want? His attention has been centered around you. We've been assuming it's because of your position with the embassy, but he had an affair with your girlfriend and now he thinks you're interested in me. He even asked me about our relationship at dinner. So what does he have against you personally?"

Harry tried to give the question the consideration it deserved, but it was hard when his head was busy fabricating images of Lies with another man. And not just any man—someone he had such little respect for. That was the second kick straight to the groin.

"Mutual dislike would be my best guess."

"Bernard Vanderloord doesn't like or dislike people," Lies replied. "He either has a use for them or he doesn't. He thinks everything through. If he's after your connections he's going about it the wrong way, so that can't be it—he's trying to push your buttons, not get on your good side. Why would he do that? What would he gain?"

"I have no idea," Harry admitted. "Maybe he thinks I have great taste in women."

Lies went very quiet, sending the conversation in a direction he hadn't intended and should have avoided, but a childish part of him had wanted to hurt her too. Because he really was hurt that she'd kissed another man.

No one could be more surprised about that than he was.

"Are we so much alike? Alcine and me?" she finally asked.

"You have nothing in common," he relented. If anything, they were polar opposites—except when it came to Vanderloord.

"Did Alcine pursue Bernard or did he pursue her?"

"I couldn't say." Harry hadn't wanted to know. He hadn't cared enough to find out. All that mattered was that he and Alcine were finished—as they should have been a long time before the affair ever began.

"But the Albanian diplomat's wife went after him?"

"I'd have to say yes on that one."

"I'm missing something."

"It's late," Harry said. "Figure it out in the morning."

A taut string of tension quivered through the telephone line between them. "You're angry."

He hadn't kept as tight a grip on his hostility regarding her methods of interrogation as he'd thought and he didn't like giving her more power over him than she already had. "Why should I be angry?"

"Because of a little kiss that meant nothing to me. This is a part I'm playing."

Damn right he was angry and she'd just tossed fuel on the fire. He'd been down this road with a woman before and he wasn't traveling it again. "If you could have avoided it, would you?"

There was a long stretch of silence. "Probably not."

She had to pick now to be honest. The knot in his stomach returned. "Why did you tell me about it then?"

"I'm not like your ex-girlfriend. I don't sleep with two men at the same time."

"To be fair to Alcine, she didn't either." He rolled to his side, taking the sheets with him, the phone's receiver pressed to his ear. He tucked the pillow beneath his head and his elbow beneath the pillow. He should let this go and hang up now. Since he couldn't, he had to address it. "Tell me something. When it comes to this role you're playing, where do you plan on drawing the line?"

"It was just a kiss, Harry."

If it had been the casual kind exchanged between friends she would never have mentioned it to him. Therefore, it mattered.

On the other hand, it also mattered that she'd told him. He couldn't decide how he felt about it that she had. Angry, yes. Jealous, without a doubt.

But relief factored in too, even though he'd spent the past two days reassuring himself there was no relationship developing between them. Since she'd called him at one o'clock in the morning, apparently to ease her conscience, he could safely assume that the other night hadn't been casual for her either, adding another layer of complication to where they were headed.

"Let me put it another way," he said. "Where do you draw the line with men, period?"

"You're blowing this out of proportion."

He doubted it. Lies had a lot of natural confidence in herself and it went a long way. But at twenty-eight she was eight years younger than he was, and in some areas it showed. If he looked back to where he'd been in his career at the same point she was at now, it was easy to see that while she might be good at what she did, she wasn't as experienced as she tried to pretend. She'd already made a mistake once by mixing business and pleasure with some man named Michael. She was making a far greater error with Vanderloord, who had twenty years on her, now.

Harry didn't know if he and Lies were in the first fragile stages of a relationship or not, or if he was simply another one of her bad decisions, but no matter how big the attraction between them became—and to him it was already out of control—if she went too far with Vanderloord, he suspected he'd never get past it. But were they on the same page as to how far too far was? Who got to decide?

"I'm going to put it in perspective for you," he said. "If you think he's trying to get to me through you for some reason, then that kiss was just the beginning—and since you're the one who's been encouraging him, you aren't going to be able to avoid the next move he makes. Trust me. It will be more than a kiss. So. Again. At what point are you planning to draw the line?"

"If I'd wanted a lecture I would have called home. You could try being helpful instead," she complained. There was a long, drawn-out sigh on her end. "How do I fix this?"

Harry's heart lightened. She'd recognized her problem and come to him for help in figuring out a solution. That was why she'd called him in the middle of the night. Anger still roiled like an angry sea inside him, but more at the situation now and less so with her. He'd wanted to know who she really was and this was a start.

What he wasn't as clear on was what she believed her mistake to have been. Was she suffering from a moral dilemma or a professional one? Maybe a little of both?

"Since you think Vanderloord is trying to get at me for some reason—" although Harry couldn't begin to imagine what it might be "—we could try a combination of Plan A and Plan B. Let him think the attraction is mutual and we're sleeping together."

"That shouldn't be difficult since we are."

An image of her flushed cheeks and heavy-lidded eyes, and the soft sounds she'd made as she came with him buried inside her invaded his thoughts. So did his resolve to end things between them. He'd been the one to initiate sex, yes, and he was willing to admit his mistake, because they couldn't continue this way. He didn't do casual.

"About that," he began, trying to figure out the most tactful way to handle breaking up a relationship that might not exist. Over the phone wasn't ideal, but might well be safest. "We need to talk."

"Another brilliant idea, since it's too late for you to come over here now." Her voice went husky with approval and a smoldering of heat. "We can make do with right where we are. Are you in bed?"

"Yes," Harry replied, left in the dust by the about-face in the conversation, "but I don't—"

"I'm not wearing any panties," she interrupted him. "Are you naked too? I'm touching myself. The same way you touched me. Mm. I like it, Harry." He heard a tiny hitch in her breathing, and a faint edge of delight to her tone that he fought to ignore, even as his mind's eye drew him pictures of what she might be doing. "I have a finger inside me and I like it so much. Tell me how you'd like to be touching me if you were here."

This wasn't going to happen. He was being manipulated—diverted away from a topic Lies no longer wished to discuss—and he knew it. He should put an end to this now. And yet it was oddly exciting. "I am not having phone sex with you."

"Then I'll have to do this alone, although it won't be nearly as much fun. You're welcome to listen to me pleasure myself though." A soft, dramatic sigh filled with promise had the blood rushing from his head to his treacherous groin. "But wouldn't you like to know how I'd be touching *you* if we were together? Because I'd be using my tongue, Harry. I'd be licking you. Tasting you. I'd have you in my mouth and I'd suck on you. I'd slide my tongue around the rim of your…" She stopped. "What euphemisms do you want me to use? Or are you more of a clinical kind of person? Forget that. I already know you are. But I'm not, so I'm going to say 'pleasure rod.'" She made a soft, humming sound of enjoyment that had his blood pressure soaring. "Because it's certainly that."

He was shocked. Fascinated. And, no matter how hard he fought it, hopelessly aroused even as the ridiculousness of what they were doing hit home. No matter how improbable it seemed, even to him, Canada's defense trade commissioner to the Netherlands was having phone sex with a CSIS intelligence officer. What should have been a turn-off only served to excite him more. How did she do this to him? How did she make him forget every ounce of decency he owned?

"Dear God. I hope my phone's not being tapped," he ground out, giving in.

"It's not. I checked." Another rustle of sound, one that sparked his overactive imagination, and he ran through all the possibilities of what she might be doing to herself in his name. "Are you touching yourself, Harry?"

"No." His throat had gone dry and his response came out hoarse.

"Liar."

Maybe he was. Maybe he did have his fist around his junk and was pumping it hard. No one could blame him. She had him hot and close to the edge and all she was doing was talking.

Sweat rolled down his back. He had to regain control of this situation, or as much of it as he could. Barring that, he sure as hell wasn't embarrassing himself first. Not when she could be faking. He wouldn't put it past her if she were.

Which just made it hotter. He gritted his teeth against the pending eruption.

"I'm touching myself," she whispered. "I'm rubbing my clit and I'm imagining it's your fingers on me. I love what you're doing to me. I—I'm going to…"

A soft cry followed by short, breathy pants sparked a response he had no hope of controlling.

"Goodnight," he said firmly, and hung up the phone.

CHAPTER TEN

SEXUAL SATISFACTION MINGLED WITH relief as Lies, too, hung up the phone, the pleasure of her release magnified by the sounds of Harry's hoarse breathing that said he was coming with her, or at least on the brink.

She wasn't proud of using sex against him—although phone sex with Harry had the potential to be almost as good as it was in person if he'd learn to relax—but the chill in his tone and the polite, professional control throughout their conversation had carried an ominous portent.

She should have let him end things. He was far too judgmental, and not only when it came to her work. People often got carried away and did things they regretted and she was no exception. She liked to have fun. She wasn't perfect and she refused to apologize for a kiss she hadn't instigated. She didn't owe him any explanations. This had been a courtesy call, at least until it morphed into sex.

And yet she'd known in her heart that kissing Bernard was something he would strongly object to. Guilt had slithered into her soul and given her conscience a swift kick in the ass. She had no desire to hurt Harry. He'd been cheated on once. If she'd been in his shoes and he'd kissed another woman after a night of great sex with her, she would have been angry too.

It all changed nothing. She was still going to dinner with Bernard. It was her job and she had no real choice. There'd be other people present so she'd be safe enough. Besides, Harry had given her a viable solution for avoiding any further advances. If Bernard tried to take things to the next level—and she conceded that he probably would—then she was going to develop the worst case of unrequited love he'd ever witnessed and cry on his shoulder over Harry.

Which brought her back to the reason she was in the Netherlands in the first place. She hadn't lied to Harry when she'd said she believed Bernard was only interested in her because he had a vendetta against him. Bernard was a successful, attractive man who didn't need to pursue an entry-level embassy employee fresh out of college no matter how cute he found her. The affair with the Albanian diplomat's wife could be explained. The affair with Alcine could be too, if taken at face value. The two women shared a type—both were dark, very beautiful, and polished in a way only supermodels could be. They screamed expensive. But add Lies into the mix?

Not a chance. The only thing Lies had in common with either woman was Harry. So what might honest, upstanding Harry Jordan have done to anger a man who was essentially a crime boss?

She checked the time. It would be eight o'clock in the evening in Ottawa. She should check in with John Carmichael and see what he thought. He might have insights that would offer an explanation.

John answered on the second ring. "Marlies. I was wondering when I might get another update from you. How was the expo?"

"Enlightening." This wasn't the first conversation they'd had since she'd arrived in The Hague, but she finally felt she had something worthwhile to discuss. "I met the Canadian trade mission delegates today. One of them has a connection to Vanderloord that could prove of interest."

She told him about Mike Freeland and how he'd gone to university with Bernard, and of his meeting with a Ukrainian helicopter company. "I didn't find out who Vanderloord went to that expo to meet with though. He's very careful with his business in public. We shared a table at dinner with other expo attendees and he's great at small talk, but he wasn't at all interested in them. Whatever his agenda, it wasn't about networking." She told John that she was supposed to have dinner with Bernard and a few private guests at his home. "Hopefully, I'll learn more."

"Here's what we know to date," John said slowly. "Help me follow the train of events. One, Vanderloord hit our radar because of another old classmate of his from McGill by the name of Marc Leon Beausejour. Another officer has been tracking Beausejour since March. He found out that Beausejour is—or once was—a good friend of the Canadian Minister of National Defence.

"Two, a software engineer working on a top secret drone project for a defense contractor here in Canada had her email hacked through the Russian Business Network. She traced the hack back to the Minister of Defence's official office here in Ottawa, but not who it went to within the department. Shortly after her contact list was stolen a nuclear physicist working on that same drone project turned up dead in London. The nuclear physicist also once worked in the Netherlands.

"Three, Vanderloord told you he got into the import-export business with former classmates right after he graduated from McGill law school. Those former classmates are first-or-second generation immigrants with family connections in their countries of origin.

"Four, Vanderloord, whose legitimate business is shipping, was at an international helicopter expo. Since helicopters are used for ship-to-shore transport, that's not so unusual. However, those drones also have ship-to-shore capabilities. That's another piece to consider since we have reason to believe, from information Harry supplied us with, that Vanderloord is moving stolen Canadian military weapons systems parts across EU borders using a hawala system of exchange. Also based on information Harry provided, Vanderloord has a connection to goods being transported into Russia. And coincidentally we have a Canadian lawyer, another former classmate of Vanderloord's, who's part of a shipping trade mission delegation to the Netherlands. That lawyer was anxious to attend the same helicopter expo as Vanderloord, where he met with Ukrainian representatives. The lawyer is someone I need to have investigated.

"All of which," John concluded, "makes Vanderloord of considerable interest to CSIS. All roads lead to Rome. It doesn't, however, give me enough to connect the defense minister to the supply chain for those missing weapons systems parts. The military will already have their intelligence officers conducting an internal investigation, but I'm reluctant to open a dialogue with them just yet. They'd file a report as part of CYA if I did, and I want to keep as much information off the radar as possible."

CYA was an acronym that stood for *cover your ass* and the military was big on it. They had their own justice system—which was also overseen by the Minister of National Defence—and no one in their right mind would risk having to stand before one of its tribunals to justify their actions.

"Can the business Vanderloord says he started with friends straight out of McGill be investigated that far back?" Lies asked.

"Vanderloord does seem to have stumbled on an intriguing business model at a fairly young age," John mused. "I wonder how legitimate it was in the beginning. If they registered it as a company or ran it informally as a hawala system even then. The government is getting better at tracking those types of businesses, but back in the early nineties it would have been like a license to print money to anyone with the connections and *cojones* to pull it off. And now I'm curious to find out if that lawyer has family in the Ukraine."

"Would a Ukrainian connection have been of any use to anyone running a hawala back in the early nineties?" Lies asked.

"Yes. The Cold War officially ended in 1991 and Canadian trade relations with the Ukraine started up again in the mid-nineties. Because of our high Ukrainian immigration population, old family ties were quick to reemerge." She could imagine John frowning as she waited for him to work it through. "What surprises me is that young men in their twenties would have been shrewd enough to see the opportunities."

"They likely had those opportunities pointed out to them by people with more experience. Or had family back home who took advantage of their second-generation or landed-immigrant status," Lies said. She came from an immigrant family. She knew firsthand how hawala systems worked. Money and goods crossed borders between family members all the time.

"We're doing a lot of speculating." The silence

following the statement told her John was thinking. "Freeland might give us the link we're looking for. If he has it we can find it. But it's not illegal to have family and friends. When you go to Vanderloord's home for dinner, don't forget to plant a listening device. He's not dealing directly with the minister. So who's acting as their go-between?"

"Are we still ignoring Vanderloord's other activities?" Lies asked. Harry expected Bernard to be arrested. She'd love to do that much for him at least.

"For now. He's pivotal to tracking our missing military parts, Lies. Who knows where his dealings might lead? First we take down his connections here in Canada. Someone's authorizing the movement of those parts out of the country. After we do that, we'll see if Vanderloord remains valuable to us."

"I have another question for you." Lies told him her theory that Bernard had a personal grievance against Harry. "He's pushing Harry for some reason. You know Harry. Why do you think that might be? What reaction is he trying to get out of him?"

"I haven't the faintest idea," John admitted, sounding troubled. "Whatever Vanderloord hopes to accomplish, it's safe to say that he's going to end up disappointed. Harry's as straight as they come. Keep an eye on it though. Harry's a rising star in diplomatic circles. I don't want his career touched by this in any way. He's going to be useful to us someday."

So much for any possible insights John might have.

Long after the call ended, Lies lay awake in the dark. Harry had gone to CSIS with a problem. CSIS was dealing with it, but not in a way that he'd consider helpful. Bernard would go about business as usual and Harry would go about embassy business believing that

CSIS—meaning Lies—hadn't gathered enough information to shut Bernard down, when the exact opposite was true.

It would be far worse if he found out that CSIS had deliberately let Bernard walk. She got that the bad guys didn't always get what was coming to them and could shrug it off. Intellectually, Harry got it too. But in his case, because it had become personal, righteous anger would eat at him every time he looked at Bernard.

John didn't know Harry well at all if he thought he would ever do favors for CSIS again. Not after they'd double-crossed him this way.

And by "they" she meant "she." Because she'd let things become personal between them.

Harry liked the routine of drinking his coffee and opening his mail every morning, making a few early calls to countries in other time zones, and generally putting his world into order.

This day, however, was off to a gray and dreary beginning. Rain pounded against the window of his office, streaming down the glass and blurring the outside world, ruining what little concentration remained to him. He couldn't absorb what he was reading, poring over the same paragraphs multiple times. He'd discovered his coffee cup empty and had no memory of drinking it. Making phone calls was pointless because he wasn't paying attention to whoever he called.

Instead, he waited for the cheerful sound of Lies's voice as she greeted the other staff in the office, then the rapid click of her heels on the tile floor as she raced for her desk because she was always seconds away from being late. She'd turned his world upside down.

So much for calling it quits. He wasn't finished with her.

He tapped the end of his pen against his desk. He wasn't over the kiss she'd shared with Vanderloord by any means, but was willing to accept that it had meant nothing to her. The uncertainty over how he'd be able to face her after phone sex had become the bigger dilemma. He had no point of reference.

God, he really was dull. How he must entertain her. He'd lost all control in this relationship, whatever it was, and it was time to reclaim it. The next time they had sex it would be with full body contact. They would do things his way. He'd take it slow and be thorough, and there'd be no question as to how good it had been. Not for either of them. They'd both be present in the same room and would know.

She arrived three minutes after the hour and rushed past his open door without pausing. Disappointment warred with relief. All of the things he'd rehearsed in his head to say to her disappeared.

When ten o'clock rolled around and she hadn't stopped by his office to torment him, he knew something had to be wrong. It wouldn't have anything to do with last night because she wasn't at all reticent when it came to sex. If she had complaints she'd have barged in here first thing and told him where his performance was lacking and given him tips for future reference.

If she wasn't coming to him, then he'd go to her.

She was at her desk, sorting through a stack of invoices. Blond curls, dampened by the rain on her walk to work, had dried into a disorderly mass that had him wanting to dig his fingers through them. She looked up when he approached. A smile shone from her brilliant blue eyes, stealing the gray from the drab morning. She seemed happy enough to see him, and not at all awkward after their late night conversation, so why hadn't she stopped by his office?

On closer inspection, as he was trying to decipher what her uncharacteristic restraint might mean, he noticed the faint bruises shadowing the delicate pale skin beneath her eyes and realized he was an idiot. Not everything in her life was about him. She hadn't called him after midnight because she longed to hear his voice or thought it might be amusing to drive him insane by telling him how she'd kissed another man. She'd been going over her notes from the expo and her dinner with Vanderloord. She did an honest day's work for him here, then had her own investigation to consider. The stress of holding down two jobs—of leading a double life—was beginning to wear on her. Last night would have offered her little more than an entertaining and somewhat safe diversion.

He couldn't decide which of them he felt sorrier for.

"Go home," he said abruptly.

Her smile faded. She canted her head to the side as if she'd misheard him. "I don't understand."

Of course she didn't. No matter how it sometimes seemed to him, she wasn't a mind reader. "You worked extra hours at the expo yesterday. You've attended several evening events on the embassy's behalf already. You've earned a break."

"I'm fine," she assured him.

She wasn't.

He made a rash decision. "I have a dinner meeting this evening and I'd like you to go with me. Go home, get some rest, and I'll pick you up at six. Cocktail attire," he added.

"It's not on your calendar." Faint exasperation tinged with long-suffering humor colored her expression. "Let me show you again how to add meetings into your phone."

He hated that app. He didn't need the constant reminders chirping at him. "This was last minute."

She looked at the stack of invoices, which likely weren't helping to keep her awake, then up at him. "If you're sure…"

"I am."

She began gathering her raincoat and purse and he returned to his office.

Despite all the flirting. The teasing. The sex. He didn't *know* her. He wanted to.

He had a phone call to make and a favor to ask.

The restaurant, a converted nineteenth-century carriage house formerly owned by the Dutch royal family, now belonged to a good friend of Harry's.

Marlon, a short, round-bellied man, had thick, salt-and-pepper hair and a clean-shaven, baby-like face. He greeted them at the door, clasping Harry's hand, his eyes wandering over Lies in a highly appreciative manner that didn't bother Harry in the least. Marlon was happily married and Lies did look stunning. She'd tidied her curls but hadn't bothered to try and tame them, a look that he liked. She wore a trace of makeup around her eyes, emphasizing their size and vibrant color, but taking nothing away from their natural beauty. Her lipstick was a dark shade of pink well suited to her light complexion.

She'd opted for the standard little black dress, a safe

choice for an unknown venue, although it had a few departures from the typical conservative features. Harry viewed the anomalies with appreciation as they were escorted through the main level of the restaurant, Lies a few steps ahead. The dress had a high neckline and long sleeves, but the back was nonexistent, plunging in a wide vee from the rounds of her shoulders to her waist. The hem of the tight skirt touched a conservative inch above her knees. In the back however, the slit meant to facilitate walking hadn't taken bending over into consideration.

Although Lies bent over while wearing that dress certainly had Harry's consideration. He imagined her hands gripping the back of the sofa in his flat while he stood behind her, spreading her thighs, making her ready for him with deft strokes of his fingers. Perhaps his tongue.

He dragged his attention back to the moment. That was for later. He had other plans for the first part of the evening.

They climbed a spiraling central staircase to Marlon's personal table. He was speaking to Lies in Dutch, taking for granted by her appearance that she was a national. She laughed at whatever he was saying, her rapid-fire response too fast for Harry, with his limited understanding of the language, to follow. All he caught was *Canadees*, which meant Canadian, and a reference to Frisians.

"He said my accent is charming and asked where I'm from," Lies translated for Harry. "I told him I'm Canadian but my family is from Friesland."

"And I said we won't hold her family against her and she's welcome here regardless," Marlon interjected. "I'm usually very good at identifying what part of the country people are from. Her Dutch is impeccable but the hint of Canadian and Frisian in her accent made it difficult to place." He held out a leather chair for Lies so she could sit down, then patted Harry on the shoulder. "Enjoy yourselves. I'll be your waiter for the evening. Let me treat you to a bottle of my favorite wine."

A silk screen separated their table, which overlooked the marble kitchen and its industrious staff, from the rest of the restaurant to give them an illusion of privacy. Lights made of Austrian crystal gleamed from low recesses in the high-ceilinged walls. Windows of distorted glazed glass extended from the ground a level below them to the ceiling a level above.

"Where are the others?" Lies asked as Harry took a seat across from her. She examined the table. There was enough room for eight but only settings for two. Candles and a centerpiece of orchids spoke of intimate dining. "Are we the first to arrive?"

"There aren't any others. They all canceled."

Lies leaned toward him, her elbows on the table and her chin on her linked fingers. She arched a brow. "Harry. Is this a seduction?"

This was more like her. Intent on unsettling him. He might not know her as well as he should, given the things they'd done together, but he was on to her game.

The problem was that he didn't mind when she won. And that he didn't like for her to play it with others.

"If you behave yourself, yes," he said. "Otherwise, it's a business meeting that went sideways thanks to my inability to master the meeting app on my phone."

"How would you like me to behave?"

She made her words, so innocent when taken at face value, sound suggestive, giving him visions of her under the table with her head between his legs. His fly was open and she had her mouth on his erection. Already, it was shouting out for her attention.

He was a fine one to talk about boundaries. He'd thought phone sex had stretched his, but this...

He reined in his aching erection with ruthless determination.

"At least until after dinner," he said, earning a smile that suggested she knew where the evening was headed and couldn't wait for the next stage, making his own impatience soar.

He was saved by Marlon, who brought the bottle of wine he'd promised, then returned a short time later to take their order.

The evening passed quickly enough as they chatted about a number of benign topics. She enjoyed politics and sports, and interestingly, had a keen memory for statistics. Yet even though she appeared to be having a good time in his company, and he enjoyed being in hers, he could tell that something continued to bother her and he wanted to know what it was.

He'd planned on taking her to his place after dinner. Instead, as they said good-bye to Marlon at the door and walked into the evening, Harry made a slight change to his agenda. If they went to his flat there would be no more talking.

The rain that had poured buckets all day was finished, leaving the night air clear and warm, and smelling of earth and the approach of autumn.

"Let's go for a walk," he said. He paused. She was wearing heels. "Your shoes. Are they comfortable?"

"They're fine."

The foundations of the buildings along the street, including Marlon's restaurant, formed an integral part of the canal system, and acted as a buttress. In the old days deliverymen would arrive at the businesses and households by boat and unload their goods at service doors opening directly onto the water.

A block down the street, beside one of the bridges that

crossed the canal, was a boat launch for day tours. The tours had ended hours earlier. The bleak weather would have been hard on business. As Harry had hoped, however, a few of the boatmen still lingered, tidying their craft in preparation for the next day's tourist operations.

After a brief negotiation, and an exchange involving several hundred euros, he'd secured a private ride. The boatman took his position at the wheel in the bow. Harry escorted Lies to the stern where they could sit in solitude and speak without being overheard. They sat side-by-side, close but not touching. The low, vinyl-cushioned benches were comfortable enough to make the ride pleasant as they pulled away from the dock and plodded up the canal under the blanket of night. City lights glittered along the banks, interspersed with the beams of slow-moving traffic and bicycle headlamps. Shadowy branches of weeping trees dipped downward to stroke the water's black surface, which rippled like a washboard from the boat's lazy passing. The moon was out, a pale wafer in the velvety sky, but the haze of smog and the glare from the city blocked any stars from view. The air was chillier on the water so Harry shrugged out of his suit jacket and draped it around her shoulders.

Their captain kept his back turned to them, earning his tip. The drifted along in silence, the motor chugging and the wooden floorboards humming beneath their feet. Lies didn't speak, not even to tease him, and he found that he missed it. There had been enough casual conversation between them throughout dinner.

"Why did you sleep with me?" he asked. "Why the phone sex last night? Am I that much of a challenge to you?"

"Absolutely," she replied, without any hesitation.

Well. That took the wind from his sails.

"And I'm a challenge to you," she continued. "So I could ask you the same questions, but why bother? We're both in this for pleasure. The whole evening has been wonderful. But I would have slept with you even without dinner and a boat ride, as nice as they are." She placed her hand on his thigh next to hers, tilting her face toward his. They were very close to eye level. "All you had to do was ask."

He disliked her thinking that he was only interested in her for sex. He disliked it even more that it was all she wanted from him. They had little else to offer each other however. They agreed on that much at least.

"I am asking," he said. "This time I'm using a gentleman's approach."

"And it would be difficult to resist, assuming I wanted to, which I don't." She inched her fingers higher. "But don't you ever get tired of always being so polite?"

He rubbed the back of his neck rather than slide his hand into the front of her dress as he'd like to, and tried to tame an erection that was rapidly becoming a permanent affliction when he was with her. "Groping each other in a car or on a boat in front of an audience is polite? Making so much noise that the neighbors are banging on the bedroom wall in the middle of the night is polite? Phone sex is polite?"

"I was there too, and I wasn't complaining. Don't you want it to be, I don't know..." She shrugged. His jacket slid off her shoulder. "Uninhibited? Daring? To go wherever your imagination takes you? Us?" She leaned closer and tugged at his tie with her free hand. "Take me home. Then tell me what you want me to do to you, Harry," she whispered, her breath warm on his throat, and he swallowed. "Better yet, make it an order. Trust me, I wouldn't complain about that either."

CHAPTER ELEVEN

HE TOOK HER TO his place.

Lies was surprised by his choice of residence, although not so much by the luxury of it—which was significant—as by the location. It wasn't far from the beach in Scheveningen, maybe ten minutes on foot, in an area that was upscale and decidedly hip. He was neither of those things. She'd assumed he lived closer to the embassy and his work.

"I like the ocean," he replied when she said so.

He'd grown up in Nova Scotia, she'd learned over dinner. His mother still lived in Halifax, the capital city, with three pugs and a cat she'd named after her son. That was all the family he had. Hers, by comparison, was enormous.

Yet another area in which they differed.

He parked in a designated spot on the street. They walked the flight of stairs to the second level. His door opened onto an enormous room that took up half the floor of the building. Pot lighting arced along the edge of a ten-foot ceiling where it met a rounded wall of curtainless windows. The top halves of the windows were crafted of colored glass.

Harry didn't turn on the lights, but let what filtered in from the city illuminate the spacious room. A low leather sofa divided the dining from the living area. Shadows indicated the positions of a table and chairs and, oddly enough, a piano.

Lies, however, had an interest only in Harry. From the moment they'd been escorted to the best table in the restaurant and she'd realized they were dining alone, she'd longed to straddle his lap and take him inside her right there. She wasn't normally into exhibitionism. Harry certainly was not. Not if his reaction to how they'd gotten carried away in the car after the theater was any indication. But when he'd suggested a canal ride she'd been wild with impatience and ready to reconsider. The thought of his hands on her—of having him finally inside her after waiting all evening—had left her giddy.

That same giddiness left her lightheaded now.

He tossed his car keys in a dish on the kitchen counter and loosened his tie. She'd returned his jacket to him. He eased it off his shoulders and slung it across one of the bar stools at the marble kitchen counter.

He turned to study her where she stood by the door, keeping several feet of distance between them. "If we're going to have a sexual relationship, we need to go over the rules. I don't want this spilling over into the office. And I expect exclusivity."

He said the last with a hint of a challenge, as if he dared her to argue or seek definition. She'd be offended except she understood where he came from. She'd been lied to by a lover as well. While Harry didn't have it in him to pretend to be something he wasn't, Lies had no difficulties with it whatsoever. When it came to her investigation she would lie to him if she had to.

But never about what they did together in private.

Intimacy required honesty. And trust. Those two things went both ways. Therefore she had a rule to remind him of too. "What we do when we're in bed together is separate from our careers. There's to be no pillow talk about work."

"Come here," he said.

She felt a rush of excitement at the command in his tone. Up until now she'd kept her sex life conservative. There'd be no need of safe words with Harry. Ever. And Lies was fine with that. While she wanted him to take charge, and to give her instructions, she wasn't about to start this kind of game with a man who might get carried away and not take her personal safety into consideration. But she'd spent weeks pushing Harry out of his comfort zone. Let him test hers for a change. She could tell that he'd like to.

And once committed, Harry did nothing halfway.

She stopped a hand's-breadth from him and ran her palms over her breasts and down the front of her dress. "I wore this because I thought you'd like it." She slid her arms around his neck and pressed against him. "Tell me what you were thinking when you first saw me in it. Did it make you want to touch me?"

His eyes had gone very dark. He was already hard against her. "I imagined bending you over the back of my sofa and taking you from behind."

She spun out of his arms and walked to the sofa, adding a sway to her hips. She ran a finger along the length of its low-slung back. "You mean this one?" She bent forward, grasping the butter-soft leather in both hands, and looked over her shoulder. "Like this?"

"Exactly like that."

"Is this why you brought me here? So you could take me from behind against your sofa?"

A muscle in his jaw jerked. "Yes."

The tightly-leashed arousal in his tone served to increase her boldness. "When I put this dress on, do you know what I thought you might like even more?" She arched her spine, pushing her hips upward in an invitation that wasn't meant to be subtle. "What I'm wearing underneath it. Do you want to find out what that is?"

She tracked his movements as he crossed the room. He looked so staid. Refined. Until she took in the intentness of purpose in the set of his mouth. Anticipation had her damp and ready for him.

He stopped directly behind her. He skimmed a palm up the back of her thigh and under her skirt, then over one bare cheek. "My God. You aren't wearing any underwear." He sounded as if he were strangling on a mixture of fascination and shock. "You walked around all evening like this?"

"You could have had me on the boat if you'd bothered to try."

"Hold still."

He dipped a finger inside her, then a second, and began to work her into such a complete state of arousal that obeying his command to remain still soon became impossible. She rocked against the heel of his hand.

"Do you like that?" he demanded. "Do you want more?"

"Yes," she cried.

He pushed her skirt around her waist, exposing her bottom half to the air. She felt something warm and damp replace his fingers and she gasped. Harry was licking her, thrusting his tongue in and out of her, and it felt so good she was shaking. She lifted her hips, thrusting against his mouth and his tongue, and within seconds, she came. She collapsed against the back of the sofa, a quivering mass of boneless satisfaction.

He gave her no time to recover. The soft rasp of a zipper reached her ears.

"Turn around," he said. "Kneel in front of me."

She did as he told her. He had his pants around his ankles, his erection jutting toward her face. He put both hands on her head, his fingers knotting in her curls. "Take me in your mouth. Suck me. Do the things to me you talked about doing last night. And what you were thinking about doing."

Her whole body throbbed with an eagerness to please him the way he had her. She traced the vein on the underside of his erection with the tip of her tongue. He hissed in a breath. His fingers tightened. She cupped his sac with one hand, then guided him into her mouth with the other. She worked her lips around his rim, sucking gently, her fingers stroking his length lightly.

"Stop. I'm going to come if you don't."

She ignored that command, instead working him harder, taking him deeper into her throat until he was groaning with pleasure. His hips jerked and his legs stiffened as he exploded. "*God*, Lies."

She had her hands on his thighs and she sat back on her heels, satisfied with herself in a way she couldn't begin to explain. She'd never let a man come in her mouth before.

His legs were trembling. He tipped her face upward and stooped to kiss her, his mouth hot and fierce. "I can't believe you let me do that."

"I already gave you permission to do what you want. If it's something I won't enjoy or I'm not comfortable with, you'll be the first to know."

They were both only half undressed. Lies's skirt was bunched around her waist. Harry's pants and boxer briefs had been kicked aside and his shirttail hung around his naked thighs. His tie was askew and he was breathing hard. The refrigerator kicked in, its quiet hum the only other sound in the room.

He took her by the elbows and lifted her to her feet.

"That was to take the edge off," he said. "We're just beginning. Take off your clothes."

All she had on was her dress. It unzipped at the side. She peeled the tight sleeves off her arms and dropped the dress to the floor. She stepped out of it.

She loved that Harry was getting into this. He'd seemed somewhat hesitant at first. Not any longer. He eyed her with complete self-assurance, his bold gaze skimming over her nakedness in the semi-darkness, the slight smile on his lips suggesting he liked what he saw. "Now undress me."

He had nothing on but his shirt and tie. She unfastened the buttons slowly, one by one, pressing one of her knees between his thighs so she could stand close and rub catlike against him. She had no inhibitions about her body. She had less about his. He was beautiful, solidly built without too much muscle, and perfectly proportioned. He wasn't short, but he wasn't tall either. And his feet... She ran a toe over the high arch of his instep. There was nothing so sexy as well-shaped feet on a man.

"Lean over the back of the sofa and spread your legs for me." His voice alone had her ready for him.

He dragged the tip of his finger up and down her cleft, occasionally dipping into her dampness until she was begging for him. "Not yet." He took her cheeks in his palms, spreading her wide with his thumbs. He placed himself at her entrance and slid the smooth head of his erection inside her, to the rim, then withdrew. He did it again. And again.

"*Please*, Harry."

He stopped. His voice was harsh. "The next time you decide to try phone sex with me, you're going to know how I'd be touching you."

He ran his hands up and down her back, his thumbs grazing her spine, his fingers trailing along the edges of her ribs and skimming the sides of her breasts, pebbling her skin. He eased his hands underneath her to cradle them. He squeezed his erection between her buttocks as he leaned over her, hard and insistent. His knees parted her thighs. He reached down and positioned himself, then drove his entire length deeply inside her with one hard thrust.

"*Again,*" she cried out.

Needing no more encouragement than that single plea, he took control in an unrestrained manner that she found unbearably exciting. She lifted her hips to meet each of his thrusts. The legs of the sofa lifted beneath them to thump rhythmically against the hardwood floor. He had his hands on her hips, his knees between hers, and he buried himself inside her again and again until tiny ripples of glorious sensation began in her belly, spreading down to her cleft, her body quivering with joy at her release. Her hands clutched at the cushions on the sofa, desperate for something to hold onto as she raised her hips to take Harry's length deeper. He swore as he came.

She could have purred with contentment, even draped naked as she was over the furniture. He stayed inside her for a long time, his hands idly stroking her skin. She wondered what he was thinking.

Probably that he was going to regret what they'd done in the morning. She hoped he did have regrets. It would mean he'd stepped out of his comfort zone, which in turn meant she'd be memorable to him.

He was already memorable to her. She liked the

contradictions in him she was discovering. She liked the tightly-controlled diplomat with the great sense of humor and the sexual boundaries that begged to be pushed. She hadn't yet found their limits.

Neither had he.

He withdrew, sliding from her semi-erect.

"The bedroom's this way," he said.

Now that he'd committed to an affair he was very thorough, exploring every inch of her body well into the wee hours of the morning and until she was limp with exhaustion.

She lay on her side with her hands under her cheek, facing Harry. He was on his stomach and had one arm resting over her waist. His fingers played at the small of her back, stroking her skin with a delicate touch that felt far more intimate than anything they'd done. Deep shadows, parted by a crack of light cutting between imperfectly-drawn curtains, coated the bedroom in night.

She was tired, but not too tired to talk.

"Tell me more about your childhood," she said, stretching against him. She rubbed a toe against his calf.

He turned his face toward her. "There isn't much more to tell. I wasn't a daredevil, never at the epicenter of trouble, always in the top percentile in school, and overall I was pretty dull." She could hear him smiling at her in the dark. "Not much has changed."

He couldn't possibly believe that to be true. "I have the sore spots to prove you aren't dull."

"A lot of that can be credited to you. Your enthusiasm and energy spills over."

"I didn't notice any lack of enthusiasm or energy on your part. I think it's fair to assume we're equally matched in this one area, at least."

"I suppose we are." He sounded so smug she couldn't help laughing.

"What led you into the trade commission?" she asked next.

"You mean you didn't investigate me?"

"Of course I did. You studied commerce and international business and marketing at Carleton University, then spent two years abroad as an exchange student in Stockholm. You interned for three summers with the United Nations while you did your MBA. After university, you worked for several different defense contractors in international marketing, brokering deals with foreign governments. You speak French, Spanish and Italian."

"I'm not sure how I feel about you knowing all of that."

"Those are a bunch of facts in a file that anyone could find by doing an Internet search of your name," Lies said. "I could pull them off LinkedIn. I don't know anything about you as a person."

"I could say the same about my knowledge of you— except I couldn't find anything about you on the Internet other than that bullshit story about your diplomat father."

"You know me as well as anyone does, including my mother. You simply can't accept that I really am who I appear to be because I work undercover." She kissed him, a soft brush of her lips against his. "I know one thing about you. You have trust issues."

"I suppose I do." He was quiet until the clang of a church bell, dulled by distance, pronounced the half hour. "Would you really have had sex with me on a canal boat if I'd asked?"

The answer was a resounding maybe. "What do you think?"

The sheets rustled as he rolled onto one hip. He grazed the line of her jaw with a knuckle. "I think you only said that to shock me."

"See? You know me better than you thought you did." She threw her leg over his thighs and burrowed against him. "For what it's worth though, I wanted you badly enough that we can never be sure."

His soft chuckle rumbled around her. He pressed a kiss to her forehead. "Go to sleep. It's late and I'm exhausted."

"I'm going to be late for work," Lies said. A quick glance at her watch confirmed it.

Harry had stipulated that their relationship wasn't to carry over to the office and she'd respect that. She felt a tingle of guilt that she wasn't going to tell John Carmichael, or at the very least Dan, but she planned to keep it out of her workplace too.

What was happening between them was private.

Despite the ticking clock and desire for discretion, the last thing she wanted to do was crawl out of Harry's bed. He was towel-drying his hair with brusque strokes in the adjoining bathroom. What he hid under his business suits was deceiving. Right now he had another towel around his narrow hips and looked delicious. He had strong arms and a broad chest, and buttocks well-muscled from bike riding.

He dismissed her concern with the negligent shrug of a man in complete charge of his workplace. "If anyone asks, tell them we had a breakfast meeting scheduled before I left for the airport."

She'd forgotten he had meetings in Paris that afternoon

and tomorrow. With a sigh, she threw back the bedclothes and went in search of her dress.

The car Harry had reserved to take him to Schiphol drove her home en route. He insisted on walking her to her door. An elderly gentleman wearing a black hat and carrying a hand-carved cane hooked over one arm hobbled out of the lift as they waited to get in, wishing them both a caustic *Goedemorgen* that reeked of disapproval.

Lies compared her rumpled appearance with Harry's and at this time of day, it wasn't favorable. In his usual suit and tie he looked every bit the diplomat. She could only imagine how she must look. At least no one would guess she was an intelligence officer. Her cover was safe.

"That was my neighbor," she said as Harry slid the lift door closed and they were alone in the cramped space. "First we have loud sex and disturb him. Now I arrive home in the same clothes I wore last night, and to look at you, he'll never believe you were the same man both times. I'm going to have to move."

"Moving would be an overreaction, don't you think? You're here temporarily. You can survive a few weeks of judgmental neighbors." The shifting corners of his mouth hinted at the sense of humor he possessed underneath all that reserve. "Unless he tries to purchase your services. That could prove awkward."

The reminder that she wouldn't be here forever, and the casual tone in which it was delivered, were equally as jarring as the ancient lift lurching to a halt at her floor. He could sound less accepting of their limited time frame. While they'd agreed not to become emotionally attached, they'd barely begun to explore each other physically.

Harry didn't linger. He had a driver waiting downstairs and a plane he was perilously close to missing. He placed a hand on her hip and gave her a quick kiss good-bye. "Please try not to take advantage of my absence by placing the entire embassy under surveillance. I'll call you tomorrow after my flight gets in."

His casual assumption that she would be free for him on a Saturday night had the opposite effect on her than the one it should. It warmed her, giving her a happy little glow inside that remained throughout the morning and well into the afternoon.

When her office phone rang at a few minutes before three o'clock she thought it might be him.

It wasn't however.

"You sound in a good mood," Bernard said.

She twisted the phone cord around her finger and settled into her character. "Of course I am. It's Friday."

"Let me see if I can improve on it. Don't forget that I'm picking you up at seven tomorrow night."

Her happy glow dissipated, its bubble burst by intruding reality. She'd been so looking forward to Harry's return that she'd forgotten about dinner—but building a relationship with Bernard took priority. This was her first opportunity to get inside his home and she had to plant a wire.

Optimism didn't completely desert her. Her evening with Harry could still happen. His flight wouldn't land until ten. He wouldn't make it to her place before eleven. She could be home by then.

"I'll be ready and waiting," she said.

CHAPTER TWELVE

BERNARD PICKED HER UP at her flat, but instead of heading through The Hague he took a route that led to the A4 highway and out of the city.

"I thought we were having dinner at your place," Lies said.

He checked over his left shoulder as he changed lanes, weaving through traffic. "We are. I keep a flat here to use whenever I have business in the city so I can avoid the commute, but my main residence is in Centrum Amsterdam."

A drive that took the better part of an hour.

Lies saw her plans fall apart. Planting a wire wouldn't do her much good if she and the listening device were in separate cities. Also, she'd miss Harry's homecoming later that night. Bernard would have other guests to consider and couldn't possibly have her home in time to meet up with him.

"Who else will be joining us?" she asked.

"It will be just the two of us, I'm afraid. The other couples were forced to cancel so I hope you're hungry." Not taking his eyes off the traffic, he reached across the console and touched her knee.

Her heart sank. She'd made a miscalculation. If she'd known they'd be alone at his home, and in another city to top it off, she would have refused the invitation. Her reservations had nothing to do with Harry and his disapproval—the odds in this scenario simply weren't in her favor. She was supposed to be the ambitious-but-spoiled daughter of a diplomat who was using Bernard to claw her way to the next level, but she had no clear idea of what he wanted from her in exchange and that was a dangerous position to be in.

She should tell him to stop the car and demand he turn it around.

She was too curious as to where this was headed however. Why had he arranged to get her alone and an hour away from home? Why had his interest in her suddenly ratcheted up several notches?

"What an inconvenience for you," she said. "There's no need to go to so much trouble for me. It's only dinner. We can stay in The Hague and save you two hours of driving."

"You're no inconvenience. Besides, I already had the catering arranged." He drifted into the left-hand lane and shifted into sixth gear. "You're welcome to spend the night. I have a big home with plenty of spare room. We can both return to The Hague tomorrow in time for work on Monday."

She wasn't spending the night with him, but she'd save that argument for later. He was playing a game and she was curious as to what it was and what he wanted from her. By all accounts he was well connected, so it was possible he'd found out she was with CSIS. Perhaps he was as curious as Harry as to how far she would go in order to get what she wanted.

But she couldn't shake the belief that it was Harry he

was trying to goad. Spending the night in Amsterdam with him would certainly do that.

Pragmatism pushed away any concerns she had about how Harry would react if she did. She refused to waste her limited time with him defending the decisions she made as an intelligence officer. In her line of work, there was sometimes an unavoidable blurring of the lines between professional and personal. She'd crossed them twice now—once with Michael and again with Harry— because she was human. John Carmichael had told her to trust herself and she did.

Pop music wafted from the car's custom stereo system. Bernard sang along with the latest hits as flat expanses of fields and small villages and towns sped past. The incongruity was disconcerting—and, she suspected, calculated. He too was pretending to be someone or something he wasn't, posing a challenge she couldn't resist either.

Yes. She did like this game.

Less than an hour later they took the exit off the highway and drove into the heart of Amsterdam. Bernard parked in a private lot on a shady street along one of the many canals. The street's tall, narrow row houses were constructed of sandstone and tilted at alarming angles. Dating back as many as five hundred years, they'd been built using wooden braces that had been sunk into an unstable bed of wet, reclaimed ground. Property owners, taxed on the frontage of their homes, had opted to go higher and deeper to gain more square footage of living space and this was the result. Over time, the wooden braces had rotted and the buildings shifted. Now the homes were divided into separate living units.

They entered Bernard's unit through a communal basement that contained a small lift. The lift took them to his condo on the second floor. It opened onto a modern living room with a fireplace and breathtaking view of the canal.

As she took it all in, Lies couldn't contain her admiration. "This is so beautiful!"

Bernard appeared pleased by her praise. "Let me show you around."

A narrow corridor led from the living room, past a guest bathroom and the dining area, into a kitchen outfitted in the very latest of stainless steel appliances. Antique Delft blue tiles lined one wall of the kitchen.

The dining room table had already been set for two. From a central open staircase in the living room Bernard led her to the third floor, with two large bedrooms and a shared bath. The fourth floor contained the master bedroom and an enormous private bath outfitted with a whirlpool, bidet, double sink and more of the Delft blue tiles. Outside of the master bedroom, in an open area that served as an office, a built-in desk stretched the entire width of the floor. The hipped-beam ceiling and bent walls turned the narrow windows into skylights.

Lies's pulse hammered at the sight of the computer on the desk and the papers scattered around it. This explained how Dita had come by the information she'd passed on to Harry—Bernard worked from home. Planting a listening device might prove worthwhile after all, and this could well be the only opportunity she'd get.

"The final stop on the tour is the terrace," Bernard said, heading for the staircase.

"Do you mind if I use your bathroom first?" she asked.

He paused with one foot on the bottom stair and his hand on the low metal railing. "Of course not. Join me on the roof when you're ready. I'd like to show you the view."

Inside the master bathroom, she retrieved the fine-wired device from under her skirt where she'd taped it to her thigh. It took only a few seconds for her to insert it into the space between the wooden door frame and wall. She wouldn't be able to monitor it as much as she'd like but it was better than nothing. She eyed the bidet, shook her head over the idea of it, then flushed the toilet beside it and washed her hands.

When she emerged from the bathroom she was alone. The door at the top of the stairs was open to the night. She listened but heard nothing other than the faint hum of city traffic from outside.

The papers on the desk proved irresistible. The letterhead on one piece in particular captured her attention. It was from a shell company she'd come across already when looking into Bernard's business dealings.

Shell companies weren't illegal. They had no assets and on their own were usually inoperable. That was what made them attractive to underground economies. Because they remained legal entities, money could be moved through them. She wished she could take photographs. Instead, she'd have to make do with her memory.

She'd scanned the contents of five similar pages when a whisper of movement at the top of the stairs caught her ear. A shadow filled the doorway. She didn't move from where she was, but waited for Bernard to descend the first few stairs to where they could see each other.

"I've been thinking about buying a Mac. Do you like yours?" she asked, gesturing at his computer. She hadn't disturbed the screensaver. The papers too were exactly as he'd left them. She'd been careful. "Do you do any desktop publishing with graphics? I'd like to try creating brochures for the office."

"I have a professional design program installed."

"Could you show it to me?"

He descended the stairs and approached the computer. She read nothing in his facial expression or body language to suggest he found her curiosity alarming or intrusive, although that meant little in the long run. He was a better actor than she was. And she was good.

He gathered the papers and straightened them before sliding them into a folder. He then spent the next few minutes showing her the software program he used. She caught a quick glimpse of the icons on his desktop but saw nothing other than things any ordinary business would use.

"Now," he said finally, shutting down the program and the computer with a few clicks of the mouse. "Let me show you the terrace. It's the real reason I bought this home."

When she saw it, she could understand why. A wooden fence divided the townhouse roof into quarters so that all of the owners sharing the building had their privacy. The fence surrounding Bernard's terrace was three feet high at the lip of the roof and eight feet along the other three sides. A teakwood patio set and two lounge chairs fit the space nicely. Scattered planters with shrubs provided a touch of greenery.

The view from the living room had been impressive enough. From the rooftop it was spectacular, revealing breathtaking examples of the city's eighteenth century architecture. Nearby, the Rijksmuseum's towers breached a sea of clay-tiled rooftops, private gardens, and trees.

She shivered a little. She'd left her jacket downstairs and the night air blowing off the IJ, the body of water leading to the North Sea, was crisp despite the residual heat from the concrete and brick of the city.

"Let's go see what the caterers left for us," Bernard said.

Dinner in the formal dining room was delicious. Twice now she'd been treated to gourmet cooking. She wasn't used to the decadence and could see how easy it would be for an intelligence officer to get lost in this type of game.

But by the time they reached dessert, Bernard was on his third glass of wine and the game was far less entertaining. Unpleasant certainty, along with feminine outrage, settled into her stomach. He'd had no intentions of driving her home tonight. Being over the legal limit was going to be his excuse.

The entire evening was so...calculated. If she were exactly what she pretended to be—a girl straight out of college with little experience around men much more mature than she—then maneuvering her into this situation was unforgivable of him. It was an abuse of power and she had no patience for it.

She set her napkin beside her unfinished pastry. This required a different tactic than the approach she'd been using, which would have allowed him to save face. Now the gloves were off.

"You didn't invite anyone else this evening, did you?" she challenged him.

His smooth, sheepish smile contained more satisfaction than apology. He bore the air of an unrepentant schoolboy caught red-handed breaking some minor and inexplicable rule. "No."

And yet he wasn't interested in her sexually. She was certain of it. "Why did you invite me?"

His gaze dropped to the front of her dress, which showed very little cleavage and was hardly enticing. "Is it so ridiculous to think I might be attracted to you? Is the difference in our ages a problem?"

She smothered her anger. They were still playing a game and she'd be damned if she'd lose. "Yes and no. In that order. The only attraction you feel toward me is based on whatever you believe I can do for you. What might that be?"

His eyes laughed at her, but he sounded sincere enough when he replied. "You sell yourself short, Marlies. I find you very attractive. More so by the moment. But for the sake of playing along, I could ask you questions too. Why did you allow me to bring you here? What do you want from *me*?"

Caution seized her. He knew who—what—she was. But how?

All of their prior interactions flipped through her head at a dizzying speed, leading her to a single conclusion. He had no proof, only suspicions.

She clasped her hands together and rested her elbows on the table, leaning on them so they carried her upper body weight, striving to appear relaxed. An unruly ringlet tickled her right eyebrow as she grasped at bits and pieces of dinner conversation from evenings on her family farm so as to craft a plausible story.

"I have a friend in Ottawa," she said, "whose family are horse people. He believes he can make money by purchasing embryos from Vyatka breeders in Russia, transferring two or three at a time into more common brood mares, then flying the brood mares to Canada. He ships four horses for the price of one. He offered me a percentage if I can arrange a meeting for him. I was hoping you might have connections in Russia I could use." She knew nothing of horses other than that the Vyatka was a rare Russian breed. That was why she'd added a friend to her story. If asked for details she could plead ignorance and defer them to him. However, the situation she'd described wasn't so different from how Bernard had gotten his own start in business.

His expression closed over. Candlelight sparked off the abrupt chill in his eyes. But if he had an opinion on the viability or even veracity of her supposed friend's business plan, he kept it to himself.

"My connections in Russia are useless right now. The Netherlands has imposed trade sanctions against them." He played with his half-empty glass, twirling the stem between his thumb and forefinger. "It's my turn. Why did Harry suddenly decide he needed a personal assistant?"

If he'd hoped to catch her off guard with his question he was destined for disappointment. She shrugged. "I thought it was obvious. Because my father called in a favor."

"Interesting." Bernard took another sip of his wine. He watched her closely, his eyes never leaving her face. "Does your father know that you're sleeping with Harry?"

That one did take her by surprise. She weighed the pros and cons of denying it and decided to go with the truth. Somehow he knew. And the only way he could know was if he had either Harry or her—possibly both—under surveillance. The game had become that much more challenging and she wasn't about to give ground.

"Do you always make a play for the women Harry sleeps with?" she fired back.

Bernard laughed with genuine amusement. "He told you about Alcine?"

"The entire embassy knows the story."

"Poor Harry."

"Why do you dislike him so much?" she asked, curious because Bernard didn't sound sorry for him at all.

"I don't like or dislike him. I simply have no use for men who broker deals behind closed doors."

The hypocrisy of that statement might have been breathtaking if crime bosses operated under the same set of rules as the rest of the world, but most believed they were above them and Bernard was no exception. She couldn't figure out where this conversation was headed though. Did he know that Harry had gone to CSIS? Or had he learned something from Alcine to make him so wary?

"I find that hard to believe," Lies said. "In my experience, Harry is completely honest and straightforward."

"In many regards, yes," Bernard conceded. "But I wonder what people would say if they knew that honest and straightforward Harry was sleeping with a junior staff member?"

Lies let that sink in for a moment, rolling it around in her head. She couldn't believe the conclusion she reached. "Are you planning to *blackmail* him?"

He waved that accusation aside. "As far as Harry's concerned, an office affair is hardly blackmail material. It won't harm him or his career. I am suggesting, however, that you should convince him to stop impeding my access to the primaries for the new Department of National Defence shipping contract between Canada and the Netherlands."

The light dawned. He was blackmailing her, not Harry. Now it made sense. And on behalf of her ambitious alter-ego, she was mildly insulted. She'd offered Bernard access to confidential embassy information and this was all he chose to extract from her?

"What century is this? Do you really think I care if anyone knows Harry and I are having sex? You're going to have to give me something more than a promise you won't tattle on me to my daddy in exchange."

If anything, that demand served to increase her entertainment value to him. "What would you like? Other than my connections in Russia, of course."

He was laughing at her. He thought her naïve and she had to be careful. She was supposed to be spoiled and ambitious, not stupid. Most women pursued him for his lifestyle and he was curious as to her price tag.

"I'll have to get back to you," she said.

"Surely you could find a more exciting way to advance your career than by sleeping with Harry," he prodded. "I have it on excellent authority that he's quite…average in bed."

Another statement designed to unsettle her.

"You should consider the source," Lies advised him, now burning inside with indignation on Harry's behalf. "And the fact she was willing to compare performances. Imagine what she must say about yours now that you're no longer sleeping together."

"You could find out for yourself how we compare."

He was playing with her, using a combination of shock tactics and his greater worldliness to get what he wanted, and she'd taken this game as far as she could tonight without losing more than she could afford. A glance at her watch said if she called Harry right now, she could arrange to drive home from the airport with him.

Her phone was in her purse, which she'd left on a chair in the living room.

"Thank you for dinner and your generous offer," she said, rising from the table, "but although I'm open to negotiations, I prefer to sleep with one man at a time. I'll call a taxi. In the meantime, if you can think of something other than sex as payment in exchange for my influence regarding access to those primary contractors, let me know."

Getting a call from Lies saying she'd meet him at his car in front of the Schiphol Arrivals hall, and the discovery she'd had dinner at Vanderloord's Amsterdam townhouse, hadn't put Harry in the best of good moods.

The meetings in Paris hadn't gone well either. He'd had to field questions as to how Canadian military goods could pass so easily through Europe. CSIS wasn't the only international organization with an interest in his answers.

He hated espionage. He could live without this kind of excitement.

He waited on the sidewalk for Lies. When her taxi pulled up, the short mass of blond curls and vivid blue eyes as she tipped her face upward to greet him had his heart pounding with possessiveness. The memory of her bent over his sofa, her skirt bunched around her waist and her thighs parted for him as he buried himself in her, and the breathy sounds of excitement she'd made—the throaty pleas for more—assailed him, a reminder that not all the excitement she brought into his life was so bad.

She opened her door and extended a long leg and high heel to the curb. He helped her from the back seat. The taxi had been paid by Vanderloord in advance, which rubbed him the wrong way.

She had on a far more conservative dress than the one she'd worn to dinner with him, which mollified him somewhat. The hem reached her knee and the boxy lapelled front discreetly covered her to the base of her throat. But it was difficult keeping a lid on this impotent and unrelenting jealousy he experienced every time he knew she'd been alone in Vanderloord's company. He didn't give a damn that she viewed it as work. Vanderloord wasn't in on that fact.

He wasn't going to ask her any questions until they were alone. He certainly wasn't going to say anything he might later regret. He'd take her home. Then tomorrow, after he'd had a decent night's sleep and wasn't so on edge, he'd ask for an explanation—not demand one. She never responded well when he tried to take charge.

Except in bed.

The drive to The Hague passed in silence between them, the darkness broken by splashes of sparkling light demarcating pockets of settlement off the A4, and the occasional illuminated clock face of a village church spire.

Seconds before their exit, she reached for his hand and squeezed his fingers, inching her thumb between their joined palms. The small gesture was enough to change his plans. Their time together was limited enough without him allowing jealousy to ruin it. She'd promised him fidelity. He either believed her or he didn't.

He wanted to. It was how she defined fidelity and related it to her work that gave him these gut-gnawing doubts.

When they reached her street, he grabbed his briefcase and overnight bag and got out of the car with her.

"Thank God," Lies said, eyeing the bag in his hand before smiling into his eyes. "Please tell me this time you'll stick around until morning so the neighbors will see me with the same man twice in a row."

He wanted to kiss her right there. Not because of the sex her smile promised him, but because she was fun. He liked how she made him laugh. He'd missed her as if weeks and not hours had passed. He dropped the bag on the curb and reached for her, gliding his hand beneath the tangle of curls at her nape to draw her head toward his. Her warm skin smelled of vanilla. He covered her mouth with his own, flicking his tongue between her parted lips, enjoying the taste and the feel of her as much as the lightness of heart he found in her presence.

And everything changed.

He could hold her in his arms forever, simply for the pleasure her proximity gave him. No other woman had ever brought this depth of desire for her to a relationship. He needed Lies's touch the way his lungs required air. He wanted to possess her. To own her. To keep all of this sunshine locked away for himself. He had no idea where this unfamiliar possessiveness came from. She really did bring out the worst in him. She wasn't a toy to be hoarded for his pleasure alone.

The sounds of the city slowly intruded, drawing him back to the street. A window slammed shut. A dog barked and another answered. Water lapped against the wall of the nearby canal.

"What was that all about?" she whispered when he released her, eyes wide, her soft breath stroking his cheek.

So she'd felt it too.

"Damned if I know," Harry replied, shaking inside.

Not knowing what else to do he picked up his overnight bag, but the thought of entering her flat suddenly froze his feet to the concrete. If his car hadn't already left—if she wasn't looking at him with the same confusion he knew his own face reflected—he would have gone home instead.

She grabbed his tie. "Don't even think about running, you coward. It's a Saturday night. We don't have to get up early in the morning. And I have big plans for you."

CHAPTER THIRTEEN

THE WORLD SLID BACK into place.

He had no need to run. There was no reason to feel so possessive of her. They'd agreed this was a sexual relationship, nothing more, and he should be happy about that.

But his three years with Alcine had ended in disaster and he couldn't get past that.

Lies is nothing like Alcine.

He followed her into her building. Once the door was closed to her flat, she kicked off her heels and moved into his arms. He skimmed his hands over the firm, rounded cheeks of her buttocks. If she wore panties, he couldn't tell by touch alone. The thought of possibly discovering she'd worn nothing beneath her dress to dinner at Bernard Vanderloord's filled him with dread. He wasn't confident of how he'd react, even if the omission had been planned for his benefit.

"How was dinner?" he asked, and winced as he heard the belligerence. He was about to ruin everything, and worse, couldn't stop the train wreck unfolding.

She froze. "We had an agreement. No talk about work in the bedroom."

"We can talk about work before we get there."

She sighed and turned away, padding silently on bare feet into the cramped living room, her jacket dangling from her fingertips. He keenly felt the loss of her thigh rubbing against him, but he'd started this fight.

She tossed the jacket on a stool at the kitchen counter on her way by, then sat on the sofa, crossing her long legs. She didn't bother to turn on a light. Shadows leached all color so that every object in the room took on disparate shades of gray. In the space of time it took for him to draw three breaths, she ceased being Lies, his vibrant lover, and became an intelligence officer. The transition was startling as much for its completeness as its abruptness.

"The meal was excellent," she said, "although the location came as a surprise. I thought we were having dinner with at least two other couples here in The Hague, but he claimed his plans changed at the last minute. I wanted to find out why he'd gone to so much effort to get me alone and away from home. When he tried to blackmail me into convincing you to grant him access to the primaries on a new government contract, I called you, then a taxi, and left."

She'd given him too much information all at once. His spinning head captured one item. "He tried to *blackmail* you? With what?"

"He knows we've slept together, so he has to be watching one or both of us. Logic tells me it's you, although I'm going to assume he'll be watching me too from now on. He made a comment I didn't quite understand though. He believes you're brokering deals behind closed doors. His words, not mine." Her eyes were on him, reading his reactions, every inch the professional. "Have you held something back that CSIS should know about?"

He was now on the receiving end of the accusations and he didn't like it. "Of course not."

"Is there any way he could know you went to CSIS?" she persisted.

"If he's been having me watched, then yes. I told no one I'd be in Ottawa, or why I was there, but it would have been easy enough to find out. CSIS headquarters isn't exactly discreet."

"Most informants don't walk through the front gates," Lies pointed out.

"Plenty of other people do. But if he knows I went to CSIS, then he'd also know you returned on the same flight with me. He would have no problem connecting those dots." Heavy pressure constricted Harry's chest. Lies had gone to dinner alone with a man who had connections to Russian organized crime and God knew who else. He couldn't get the dead physicist, the one with the supposedly bad heart but no pre-existing health issues, out of his head.

"I'm inclined to disagree." She patted her palm against her thigh, lost in thought. A frown marred her brow. "He doesn't act at all as if he believes I'm an intelligence officer. If anything, I'm a big joke to him."

"If he knows you're CSIS, he's not going to come right out and say so," Harry said.

She continued to frown. "I can't figure out what his game is."

He lost his last shred of patience with her. "Because this isn't a game. I know you think it is, but it's not. People have died."

She looked at him as if he'd disappointed her. "No one uses stolen military goods to build schools. A lot more people will die if we don't cut off the supply chain."

"I don't want one of them to be you."

A glimmer of his Lies returned. "You don't need to worry about me. CSIS investigates threats to Canadian security. When international situations become dangerous, we alert the CIA and have the Americans send in the SEALs to do the dirty work. How do you think they found Osama bin Laden?"

None of this was funny to him. All of the possessiveness he'd tried to submerge surged to the surface. "You're done. You've got enough information to have Vanderloord arrested. That's the last time you're to be alone with him."

He heard the sharp inhalation of her breath from across the room. "Did you just give me an order?"

He'd made a tactical mistake. She liked him giving her orders in the bedroom. Nowhere else. Yet he refused to back down. He controlled what happened inside the embassy, not CSIS. Certainly not Lies. "You aren't going to convince me to help him gain access to any Canadian defense contracts. If that's all he wants, he won't have any more use for you. You might as well call John Carmichael and tell him your investigation is over."

"Or I'll tell Bernard you fired me, and since he'd be the reason why, I'll persuade him he owes me a job. Would you like to know how I'll do that?"

He choked back his retort. She was as angry as he was and deliberately goading him. If he truly believed in his heart that she'd use sex to get what she wanted, it would be impossible for him to love her as much as he did.

He loved her.

The shock of the discovery, coming as it did on top of everything else, left his head reeling. He couldn't be in love with Lies. She was too unpredictable. Too fearless, with no sense of self-preservation. Boundaries were mere suggestions. To her, rules were made to be broken. She drove him crazy.

And she made him feel so, so alive. Every day with her promised a unique new adventure. He'd had a taste of excitement and going back to dull would never cut it. If anything happened to her, he couldn't swear he'd survive.

She'd ruined him.

"I'd better go." He grabbed his briefcase and overnight bag from the floor of the small entry and opened the door. His steps slowed despite his head urging his reluctant feet forward.

She didn't try to stop him so he left.

The insistent ringing of the phone beside her bed pried her from sleep.

Dull morning light grayed the opaque glass wall across from the foot of her bed. For one hopeful moment, as she groped for the receiver, she thought Harry might be calling to apologize.

If she'd been more awake she would have known better.

"Harry left in a hurry last night," Bernard said.

She freed herself from the sheet, its stranglehold the result of a warm room and restless night. "He didn't like that I had dinner with you and he didn't believe I had no idea we'd be dining alone. I don't think he's over you sleeping with his former girlfriend," she added, just to be mean. She was in a bad mood and didn't mind passing it on. "And I doubt very much if I'm going to be able to convince him to get you a meeting with those primary contractors. It looks like you're on your own."

If Bernard was disappointed, he didn't let on. "You genuinely like him."

That didn't quite capture how she felt about Harry this morning. "Of course I do. What's not to like?"

"I'm sorry, Lies."

He sounded sincere. She hadn't expected sympathy from him. Then again, she hadn't realized she'd need any. She stared at the thick glass blocks of the wall. She didn't know if she and Harry were finished or if he was simply being Harry and required time to think matters through, but she'd gotten one message last night loud and clear. They were two very different people, and sex, as great as it was, wasn't going to be enough to overcome that.

"Lies? Are you OK?"

She had to get her head back in the game. Bernard didn't care about her personal life, regardless of how sincere he pretended to be. She drummed up feigned indifference. "Of course. It's Harry's loss, not mine."

"I feel responsible. I promise I'll find some way to make it up to you. I've got business here in Amsterdam for the next few days, but we'll have lunch later in the week when I get back to The Hague."

He had a lot of nerve to suggest it after the way their dinner had ended, illustrating the colossal ego she was dealing with. It also meant that, despite the snafu with Harry, she continued to have something he wanted.

"I'd like that."

She set the receiver back in its cradle. After days of dancing they now had each other right where they wanted. Bernard would do her a favor that came with enough strings attached for her to owe him bigtime.

Walking out on her last night had been the best thing Harry could have done for her. It gave her a plausible reason to be bitter enough to betray him. Besides, he'd be back. She'd seen him hesitate at the door. He wasn't any more ready to call it quits than she was—although it might be best if they did. Last night was their first real fight of what promised to be many. He knew that as well as she did, which was why he'd kept going.

So why was her heart so damn sad at the thought of their affair being over?

According to the clock it was a few minutes after ten, a little early to call Yasmin on a Sunday morning. At the same time there was a good chance she'd be in.

Yasmin answered on the fourth ring.

"Why do I always fall for the wrong men?" Lies demanded.

"Beats me. I'm not the right person to ask." Her cousin's answer came out husky with sleep and pitched unnaturally low, as if she were trying not to wake someone. "Give me a second." Lies heard the rustling of bedclothes and the creak of a mattress, then the faint snick of a door being carefully closed. "OK. Tell me all about it. What did you do to make Harry mad?"

"How do you know I'm talking about Harry? And why do you assume I was the one who did something wrong?"

"Because I saw the way you look at each other. And I'm not assuming you did something wrong, I'm saying you did something to make him angry. You did, didn't you?"

Sudden suspicion interrupted Lies's desire to unload her own problems. "That had better be the soccer player and not Baart in your bedroom."

"It's neither. He's an accountant with the company I work for." Yasmin sounded self-satisfied. "He asked me out a few times and I finally accepted—which I might not have done if I hadn't met Harry and liked him so much. So see? We really do share a type. Now tell me what you did wrong so I'll know not to repeat your mistake. Then we'll figure out how to fix it."

No words came out. She shouldn't have called Yasmin. She couldn't explain to her how two parts of her life kept converging. She couldn't say how she had thought she'd loved Michael Ajam, but that the man she'd been in love with had never existed, while Harry, on the other hand, exemplified everything that Michael had turned out not to be.

She wanted to be talked out of fixing things with him, not encouraged to do so.

She'd called the wrong person.

"Go back to your accountant," she said. "We can talk later."

She cut off Yasmin's protests. Then she called Dan.

"Jesus, Lies. It's four-thirty in the morning here." He sounded annoyed and impatient, although neither was an unusual state for him to be in so she didn't let that deter her.

"I've done something stupid and I need someone to talk to. If I tell you about it, can we keep this conversation off the record?"

Three long seconds dragged by. "It depends on how stupid it is and who it involves."

"It's similar to the last stupid thing I did and might or might not involve the defense trade commissioner to the Netherlands." Perched on the side of the bed, she tensed for his reaction. It would set the tone for how much she'd feel free to say.

"What is it with intelligence officers?" Dan demanded. "Are your social skills really so poor that you can't hook up with strangers in bars whenever you need an itch scratched? Because it can't be stellar standards or morals holding you people back." He blew out a resigned sigh.

"OK. As long as the trade commissioner isn't committing any crimes and neither of you is compromising national security, this is off the record. But pretend I'm your brother and spare me the details."

A load shifted off her shoulders. Judging by Dan's reaction, hers wasn't the first phone call of this nature that he'd ever received.

She told him as much as she dared, holding back anything to do with the investigation—because John Carmichael had instructed her to keep it to herself—and the intimate details, because she didn't think Dan needed to hear how Harry had taken her from behind while she'd been bent over his sofa.

"Why are you telling me all this and not a girlfriend?" Dan asked when she finished. "Why is it my shoulder you're crying on?"

She didn't know. "You told me to protect my integrity on this assignment. I guess I needed to hear that I haven't done anything too terribly wrong."

"What are your instincts telling you? Do you think you can't do this job to the best of your abilities? Do you believe you've compromised your investigation?"

"No," Lies said. "I don't believe I have."

"Neither do I." He said it with enough conviction to ease her conscience. "Don't get me wrong. I'd rather you hadn't gotten involved with the trade commissioner. But while a lawyer might bring it up during disclosure, I doubt if it would have any real effect on the outcome of a trial. And I don't think that's why you really called me." He paused as if gathering his thoughts, or maybe he was deciding if he should voice an honest opinion. "I think you really want me to tell you to stop seeing the trade commissioner. I'm not going to do that. I want to ask you a question instead and I want you to be honest with yourself when you answer it. Is he worth sacrificing your career for? Because from what I'm hearing there doesn't appear to be any middle ground between the two of you. It sounds to me as if he hates your job."

A sick sensation clamped her stomach muscles in a vice. "What do I do?"

"Forget about whether or not he hates your job for a second and take a step back. Do *you* like your job? Would you consider taking a desk job instead?"

"I love fieldwork," she admitted. "No. I don't want a desk job. Not yet. Maybe someday. But not in the foreseeable future."

"Don't ever give up on something you love to make someone else happy, Lies. You were angry with me for telling John you'd gotten involved with Ajam. You thought I was being sexist and had double standards. Maybe I was and maybe I do. I know this sounds stereotypical, but women are more likely to give up their dreams for men than men are for women. I'm not saying to stand your ground without compromising. I'm suggesting if you want a relationship with the trade commissioner, you should start out the way you mean to continue or you'll both end up miserable. Oh, and Lies?"

"Yes?"

"If sleeping with the trade commissioner negatively impacts on this investigation in any way, this conversation won't remain off the record. And the stakes are too high for me to protect you. You understand that, don't you?"

Her fingers tightened on the phone. She'd known it when she called. "I do."

"Remember the order and priority of your commitments. Get your case wrapped up first and sort out your personal life second. That's the best advice I can give you right now."

"Thank you."

She laid in bed for a long time, mulling over their conversation. Dan was right. Until she finished this case she couldn't give Harry the consideration he deserved. She'd call in sick at the embassy for the next few days, then head to Amsterdam and eavesdrop on Bernard with that listening device she'd planted in his master bathroom.

It would give her the break from Harry her heart and mind sorely needed.

The glum Sunday morning reflected Harry's mood. He hadn't planned on waking alone. It was no one's fault but his own that he had.

He wasn't the type of man who confided the details of his relationships with women to other men.

Instead he called Alcine.

They hadn't parted on warm terms. While he deeply appreciated her confiding her concerns about Vanderloord to him, he'd been less enthused about the details of their affair and the accompanying list of his faults that she seemed to believe justified it. He couldn't say why he was calling her now.

He almost hung up. His thumb hovered over the telephone icon on his cell.

"Harry?"

He closed his eyes. "Alcine. How are you?"

Caution crept into her tone. "Is something wrong?"

Yes. I need to know I'm not a complete ass as far as women go and that I have at least a few redeeming qualities.

And he was calling an ex-lover to find out. That was

how crazy Lies made him. "No. Just checking on you."

"It's been nine months. It's a little late to be worrying about me, don't you think?" She said it without malice, simply stating a fact.

She was right and this was awkward. They weren't friends.

Maybe that was what they should have been. They'd genuinely liked each other in the beginning, but Alcine had wanted more than tepid affection. Now that he knew firsthand what they'd been missing, he no longer blamed her. He simply wished he'd been the first to find out they were finished, not the last.

"Better late than never. Believe it or not, I do care what happens to you." He really did. They'd spent three years together, not all of them bad.

"I'm getting married."

He absorbed the shock of that blunt revelation. She'd never been interested in marriage. Not with him. "Congratulations."

"I owe you an apology," she added. "There's no excuse for what I did, although I do think it turned out to be a favor in the end. For both of us."

The point wasn't worth arguing. He hadn't called her for that. "Are you happy?" he asked.

Her voice softened and warmed. "Extremely."

He waited for the jealousy to hit. It never came, making him equal parts sad and relieved. "Then I'm happy for you. Can I ask you something?"

She hesitated, her wariness returning. "Of course."

He rolled his question around in his head, seeking the best way to frame it, before giving up and tossing it at her like a live hand grenade. "Was I too possessive?"

She let out a gasp of surprised laughter. He could picture the backward tilt of her head, the length of her throat—how very pretty she was—and the memory did nothing for him. She wasn't Lies.

Her spurt of amusement turned into a sigh. "Hardly. If anything, you weren't possessive enough. If I wasn't in the same room with you, you didn't spare me a second thought. Even when I was I don't think your attention was ever completely on me. I wanted to come first in your life. The sad truth is that I didn't even come a close second."

He winced, wishing he could deny it. "I'm sorry."

"There's no reason to be. Everything's worked out for the best. I've found what I was looking for. I really hope you do too."

That was part of the problem. He hadn't been looking for anything. Certainly not what he'd found.

He made himself a cup of coffee and sat on the sofa in his living room to drink it, pondering over their conversation while watching the world news on BBC. The stark, unvarnished truth finally sank in.

He might not have been possessive enough with Alcine, but he was far too possessive of Lies. He lost his mind around her. They were no better suited than he and Alcine had been, although their differences played out in a far more destructive manner. He clasped his hands behind his head and stared into space, torn between regret and resolve.

This had to end.

CHAPTER FOURTEEN

LIES SET UP HER listening post at a small boutique hotel not far from Bernard's home. Her room, although austere and meant to be nothing more than sleeping quarters for tourists out exploring the city all day, was clean and comfortable enough for her purpose.

She had a good book with her, which was fortunate because Bernard spent little time at home on the computer or the landline next to it. By the second afternoon she was beyond bored and becoming concerned she might have to return to The Hague with nothing to show for her efforts.

And then Bernard made a phone call.

She could only capture one side of it, and she didn't understand the language he spoke, but her instincts said it was Ukrainian. She'd have to send the recording to John in Ottawa for translation to confirm that this was the connection between Mike Freeland, the lawyer, and Bernard she'd been seeking. That connection, in turn, would lead back to the defense minister. She could feel it.

"You were right," John Carmichael announced when he called her back the next evening. Lies had remained in the hotel room in Amsterdam, not yet ready to return to The Hague and cross swords with Harry. She wanted to get her job done first, as Dan had advised. "Freeland brokered the sale of weapons systems parts from Canada to the Ukraine on behalf of a third party. Vanderloord's call was to arrange for payment and delivery, and confirms the hawala system the Albanian diplomat's wife reported. Freeland, as it turns out, is the defense minister's personal attorney—on retainer, no less. And it's highly unlikely that those parts will remain in the Ukraine, or at least with that particular company. I couldn't see how a helicopter company would have a need for CP140 Aurora parts, particularly ones shipped from Canada when they could legally buy the same P-3 Orion parts directly from the original equipment manufacturer in the States, so I did a little more digging. The Ukrainian helicopter company is owned by a Russian enterprise, which in turn is owned by a dummy corporation, and—wait for it—links back to one of Vanderloord's businesses in the Netherlands."

The intricacies of Bernard's game were impressive. The defense minister's daring involvement equally so. The level of arrogance, stunning. She could only imagine what these people could accomplish if they'd harness their powers for good.

"What's my next move?" she asked.

"Now that we've established Freeland is a domestic threat to national security, we can complete the investigation of him from Ottawa. You'll finish out the next two weeks with the embassy," John replied. "I'm sure Vanderloord has been flying just under Interpol's radar for years. I don't want to take you out so abruptly that he pieces together CSIS is also now interested in him and reports his suspicions back to the defense minister. And I really don't want the minister questioning me. Once the two weeks are up you'll be transferred on paper to a

British possession in the Caribbean and disappear from the system."

Lies picked at a loose thread on the worn hotel bedspread, struggling with a sharp jolt of regret that she now had a date for saying good-bye to Harry rather than the ambiguous timeline she'd been exploiting. Sorting out her personal life was going to take no time at all. Their affair really was over.

"What about Bernard's grievance with the trade commissioner?" she reminded John, although she could see the writing on the wall for it too.

"I can't find any logic behind it. It still troubles me, but as hard as it is to believe, it might simply be a case of clashing personalities."

Translation—it wasn't CSIS's problem.

Maybe not, but it remained hers. She couldn't let it alone. Bernard claimed to neither like nor dislike Harry. He hadn't said he had no interest in him. If she left without identifying the problem, on top of CSIS not having Bernard arrested, then Harry's visit to CSIS would have gained him nothing except one more reason to remember her without fondness.

Lies had plenty of time to think about it—and Harry— on the train from Amsterdam to The Hague. She stared at the landscape whipping past, ignoring the noisy students seated behind and across from her, and rubbed at her temple with one fingertip.

Her chest ached in tandem with her throbbing temple and burning eyes. This was her second affair to crash and burn while working a case, only this time she'd fallen for a man who was exactly what he presented himself to be and she wasn't going to recover from it as quickly. She hadn't been sleeping with Harry strictly for the sex. She'd pushed him from the very beginning because she'd been drawn to him. Because being honest and straightforward didn't mean there weren't interesting layers to him for her to explore. She'd fallen in love with him the night they'd been caught making out in his car and he'd flipped off a group of boys. She would never have trusted any other man the way she did him. Not after her last gross mistake.

Two weeks. She crossed her arms, hugging her stomach.

A woman carrying a blond, blue-eyed, rosy-cheeked baby in her arms took the empty seat to her right. The baby, a girl, wore a bright blue, quilted jacket with ducks on it and shiny yellow rubber boots. Her fine, fuzzy hair stood straight up in the front and stuck out in every other direction, reminding Lies of a dandelion gone to seed. She examined Lies with wide, inquisitive eyes before gifting her with a toothless grin. Drool dribbled from a plump lower lip and down her chin, suggesting she wouldn't be toothless for long. Lies had no burning desire for children of her own, but appreciated them when she could hand them back to their parents.

"Hallo mooie meid," she said. *Hello, beautiful girl.*

The baby's mother smiled at the compliment. The two women struck up a conversation that kept Lies distracted for the remainder of the forty-five minute trip.

In the back of her head, however, she knew what she had to do and why there was no point in prolonging it. She'd tell Harry about her upcoming transfer. If he wanted to end things between them immediately, she'd begin shuffling her responsibilities to other staff members in his office, minimizing any interactions between them for the next two weeks. But if he were as reluctant to end their relationship as she was, and she believed him to be...

She couldn't allow her hopes to go there. Harry had never been about compromise.

The minute she walked through her flat door and tossed her bag on her bedroom floor, she pulled out her phone and sent a brief text. *We need 2 talk.*

His reply was immediate and equally terse. *Agreed. Be there in an hour.*

Her bell rang fifty-seven minutes later. She let him in.

His dark brown hair had been recently trimmed, the front styled so it slicked upward. Designer jeans outlined well-muscled thighs. His intent eyes, the same color as his hair, scanned her face as if committing it to memory. Her heart beat faster. She wasn't ready to say good-bye. She wanted to grab him by the lapels of his gray sport coat and drag him into her bedroom instead.

"I bumped into your neighbor on the way in and said hello." He jerked a thumb over his shoulder toward the lift, his serious expression never changing. "I told him if he hears any strange noises he should ignore them. Your reputation is saved."

His deadpan sense of humor—that most people never got to see—was another aspect of him she'd miss. The thought of never seeing him again wrenched her heart. "Are you spending the night?"

Indecision flickered, deepening brown irises feathered with gold. "No. I can't stay that long."

She shouldn't be this disappointed. "Come in and sit down so we can talk."

"I'd rather stand."

It was as if he'd seen her hunger for him and was afraid to venture too close. She was a sex partner who'd yanked him out of his comfort zone, nothing more. Any professions of love from her would horrify him. She had more pride than that.

She did.

Folding her arms across her chest, she braced her

shoulder against the wall. "Suit yourself. Consider this is my notice that I've finished my investigation. John is arranging for me to be transferred out of your office within the next two weeks."

"I see." He mulled that over. "When will Vanderloord be arrested?"

She hadn't expected that to be his first question. She'd assumed he would want to talk about their personal relationship first—that it would be equally as important to him as it was to her. Consequently, her tongue stumbled forming the explanation she'd prepared and he noticed.

"He's not being arrested, is he?"

Lying, which came easily to her in so many instances, escaped her in this one. "No. I'm sorry."

"Don't be. I know how these things work."

She wished she could tell him about the defense minister, but she couldn't. She'd never risk an investigation. Not even for Harry. "I thought you'd be angry."

"Oh, I am. Believe me. But not with you." She sometimes forgot the connections he had and how much authority he carried. He'd take his anger higher up the chain of command. He'd go straight to John. "Besides, I wanted you to be finished. Remember?"

Yes. That was what they'd argued about. So if he wasn't angry with her, and the reason they'd disagreed was now a moot point, why did he still look as if he'd bolt for the door if she made any wrong moves?

Because he'd come here to end things, even without knowing they only had two weeks remaining. Certainty was a blade of ice thrust into her heart. His explanation had better be good. She wasn't going to make rejecting her easy for him. "I gave you my news. What did you want to speak to me about?"

He shifted from one leather-encased foot to the other. His gaze, however, remained steady on her face. "It doesn't matter."

"It matters to me. If it was important enough for you to come here to tell me, then you should come right out and say it."

Harry sighed, scrubbing a hand through his hair. "I was going to tell you we shouldn't see each other outside of the office anymore."

A wave of rage breached the berm she'd erected to help her brace for rejection, swelling from her chest to her face. Spots of red light prickled at the backs of her eyes. She'd been angst-ridden over falling in love, and how hard it would be to leave him behind, and that two weeks wasn't nearly enough time to say good-bye. She'd dared to hope he might want something more and that his feelings were as invested as hers. Meanwhile, he'd been plotting how best to get rid of her.

"You're tired of the back of the sofa? You want to give your desk a try instead? I've considered it already and I'm not sure that's a good idea, Harry. The window's pretty exposed and a lot of stuff ends up on the Internet these days. Photos like that could go viral. Besides, you said you didn't want our sex life spilling over into the office."

He didn't rise to the bait she'd sprinkled like chum on the water. "Believe it or not, it's not you, it's me."

The tired cliché did nothing to dampen her rampaging fury. When people used it, the opposite was always true. "I'm trained in hand-to-hand combat. I can kill you with a jab of my finger. Do you want to stick to that story or give me the truth?"

She'd half-hoped he'd laugh at her ridiculous claim. Then they'd kiss and make up.

Instead his mouth settled into a somber expression that

gave her chills. "I hate European football. I'm not interested in nightclubs or electronic dance music. I don't have the energy it takes to keep up with you."

"You've had more than enough energy so far. If I recall correctly, we'd agreed that we're evenly matched."

"In one area," he conceded. "In others, you don't bring out the best in me. When I ask myself why, it's because of all the uncertainty that surrounds you. I don't know who you are."

Her heart bounced between hope and despair. Love was complicated and messy. It had highs and lows—and the lows he couldn't handle. Harry was all about neat and tidy emotions.

But that wasn't what had caused any real arguments between them.

"You don't like feeling jealous," she guessed, and the tightening of the fine lines around his eyes said she'd gotten it right. "Haven't you ever been jealous of a woman before?" *What about Alcine?*

"Not to this extent. Mentally, it's exhausting." His jaw worked, then hardened. "I have a question for you. Would you give up your job if I asked you to?"

Dan had warned her against traveling this road. "At the embassy? Absolutely. That place is dull."

"You know what I mean."

"Let me turn that around," she said. "Would you give up yours for me?"

"It would be foolish of me to do that. Since all I ever think about when I'm around you is getting you naked, it's doubtful we're ever going to get past the initial attraction stage of this relationship. You said yourself how important honesty is, and yet you lie for a living, so that stage would always be missing." He gave her a look that dared her to argue. "There's no security in this for me."

He meant he'd worry about who she'd be with and what she'd be doing to get information from them. She'd promised him exclusivity and he didn't trust her.

She dared him to come right out and say it. "Why don't we simply continue the sexual relationship we'd agreed on? What's wrong with exploring this stage?"

"It's not enough. I want more."

So did she. But that wasn't what he was saying. Her head got his message even if her heart wasn't as accepting. "Just not with me."

He didn't deny it, crushing her heart. "Everything is a game to you. All I am is more entertainment. You like talking me into doing things I wouldn't normally do."

That was unfair. She liked bringing out the person he was inside—the one he didn't show to the world. She'd thought he was an open book when she'd first met him. He was and he wasn't. She liked and admired the man the world saw, but it was the deeper, darker complexity simmering beneath the surface that she responded to and had made her fall in love with him. He possessed the strength to hold all of that passion in. He should be able to find the courage to let at least a bit of it out. He should be willing to fight for her. For *them.*

She'd been so sure of him. She refused to believe she'd fallen for yet another man who wasn't who or what she believed him to be.

"Are you blaming me for your loss of inhibitions or your lack of self-control?" she asked.

His face reddened. "I'm not blaming you for anything. As I said, the fault is with me." He fumbled for the door handle behind him. "I'd better go."

The door opened and closed.

She flipped the deadbolt into place, pressing her forehead against the cool wood, her palm splayed on the wall. She heard the lift grind to a stop, then a rattle of gears as it began its descent. Her anger didn't dissipate, but it mingled with other emotions now, primarily hurt and the pain of loss. Confusion as well, because he hadn't come right out and said he didn't want something more with her—he'd said honesty in a relationship was important and that she lied for a living.

But one had very little to do with the other. Deep down, he knew that. He'd brushed off being misled regarding Bernard's pending arrest. He hadn't seemed angry with her about it at all, but rather dismissed it as part of her job—which it was—leaving her with a far more consuming question. When had she not been honest with him about personal matters between them? What else had he said?

She rewound and replayed their entire conversation. He kept saying that he didn't know her, but he did. He knew her better than anyone. She'd hid nothing of who she was as a person from him.

She turned away from the door. It was too late to prove it to him. He didn't want her enough and she wouldn't beg.

On Thursday Bernard invited Lies to lunch as he'd promised. She didn't know why he'd bother since she'd already told him she'd be of no use to him.

She accepted because of an unresolved desire to discover why he had such an obsession with Harry. She didn't believe it was because of a simple personality clash, as John and Harry had both suggested.

Her morning at the embassy involved making lists and handing off her duties in preparation for her departure.

Harry had chosen to be elsewhere. The last time she'd seen him was when he'd fled from her flat. The tiny hope she'd harbored that she meant more to him than he let on flickered and died.

Hannah, the woman who'd welcomed her to the embassy when she first arrived, expressed disappointment that she was leaving so soon.

"Harry's a good boss to work for but he can be intimidating. You seem to know how to handle him. It's reassuring to us mere mortals when he acts like a human being every now and again."

Yasmin too had been disappointed when Lies called her to say she'd been transferred.

"At least visit the farm for the weekend," Yasmin urged her. "Heit and Mem—" father and mother "—will be sad if you've come all this way and never once been to see them."

Lies had spoken to them on the phone several times since she'd arrived, but until now she'd been working. Since she wouldn't be spending her last days in the Netherlands with Harry, she should really rent a car and drive to Friesland.

"Would you like to go with me?" Lies asked.

"Sorry. I already have plans."

With the accountant, no doubt. She'd have to make time to meet him before she left.

Lies kept her eye on the clock as its hands crept toward noon and her lunch date with Bernard. At ten minutes to twelve she let Hannah know where she was going and that she might be a few minutes late getting back to her desk that afternoon.

The restaurant was several blocks from the embassy gates, close enough to be popular with the staff. The day was cool and held a threat of rain. She wore a warm hand-knit sweater over slender khaki dress pants and boots and carried her raincoat in a saddlebag on her bicycle.

When she arrived at the restaurant, breathless and damp, Bernard was seated at a table near the back of the crowded room, making small talk with his waitress and flirting. The girl was dark-haired and exotically beautiful, with eastern Mediterranean looks, and much more his usual type than Lies was when she considered his personality profile. The waitress gave her a friendly welcome before moving on to the next table.

They were well into their meal of sliced ham and sweet mustard on warm bread before Bernard got to the reason behind his invitation to lunch. He reached into a pocket, then held out the wire she'd installed in his bathroom in the palm of his hand, the accusation loud for its silence.

This was an unexpected development.

"What is it?" Lies asked, rising to the challenge.

His smile thinned. "You tell me."

She opted to go on the offensive. "If you're accusing me of something, you'll have to explain."

"Very well." He snapped his fingers closed over the wire and returned it to his pocket. "I believe you planted a listening device in my home—although I can't imagine why a woman who works with the Canadian embassy would do such a thing."

It didn't matter if he knew she'd been the one to plant the wire. It was far more important he not link it to CSIS and she didn't want his suspicions heading in that direction. "Since I can't imagine it either there must be a different explanation. You wouldn't be in the habit of inviting women you hardly know to your home and encouraging them to spend the night—whether they want to or not—would you?"

He ignored the dig. "It's quite a coincidence that so

many women close to Harry also become close to me, wouldn't you agree?" He drummed long, elegant fingers on the tablecloth. "Here's what I think is happening. My private business information is being leaked to competitors. Meanwhile, Harry refuses to do business with me or recommend me to Canadian contractors. I can only come to one conclusion. Harry," he said with slow deliberation, "is using women and his position as trade commissioner to steal information from me and sell it to my competitors."

So this was why Bernard had a vendetta against Harry. He assumed that because he had no compunction about using unethical methods for personal gain no one else would either. Not to mention the elevated sense of his own worth he harbored.

Bernard's information being leaked was an interesting twist however. She'd like to know who was behind it. The scorned Albanian ambassador's brighter-than-presumed trophy wife was a safe bet. Unless it involved Canada however, it wasn't within Lies's mandate to pursue. Bernard played in a deep and murky pool. Sooner or later he'd drown in it.

"You can't possibly believe that Harry is stealing information from you," she said. "He's the personification of integrity."

Bernard patted his pocket. "This says honesty to you?"

"I have no idea what that says. I've never seen it before."

The look he gave her said fine, he'd play along. "If you want to survive in the diplomatic world, you should learn to read people. And better yet, how to protect yourself from them. Harry will put you out there Lies, and let you take all the risks, because in the end it's your neck and reputation on the line."

The ridiculousness of the situation struck her as funny. A CSIS intelligence officer was receiving advice from a crime boss on how to protect herself. She didn't know what to say or how to react, other than to inquire if he understood that this was exactly what the Canadian Minister of National Defence was currently doing to him—putting him out there and allowing him to risk his own neck and reputation.

But another part of this wasn't funny at all. She'd found no solid evidence that Bernard had murderous or abusive tendencies toward women. Dita and Alcine were both still alive. Rather, he had a casual indifference toward them. In his opinion, Lies wasn't worth any potential backlash that might arise if a woman connected with the Canadian embassy went missing.

Hopefully that same reluctance would carry over to the aerospace and defense trade commissioner too, because an uneasy crime boss with Bernard's connections was the last person Harry needed holding a vendetta against him.

She'd go to Interpol with an anonymous tip in order to protect Harry if she had to. Then they'd see how good Bernard was at protecting himself and how loyal his friends were.

Before she could think of some clever response to his helpful tips, Harry appeared in the arched oak doorway that led from the foyer to the restaurant's dining room.

CHAPTER FIFTEEN

HARRY'S CASUAL GLANCE AROUND the room halted, backtracked, and settled on her.

His gaze darkened. A thrill of desire coursed through her body before her brain reminded it that she was angry with him. This level of jealousy was ridiculous and not at all flattering, particularly since he was the one who'd ended things between them.

Also his timing couldn't possibly have been worse. She should never have told Hannah where she was going for lunch.

"Well, well," Bernard said, seeing him too. "Harry seems to have rekindled his interest in you."

Lies touched his elbow, speaking quickly so Harry, making steady progress toward their table, wouldn't overhear. "Behave yourself. You're wrong about Harry. Don't make accusations you'll regret later or you'll never get those recommendations you want."

"Good afternoon," Harry said, acknowledging Lies with a cool graze of his eyes as he reached past her to shake Bernard's hand. "What a surprise to find you both here together."

Bernard shifted into his discreet businessman guise. "I

hope you don't mind me taking Lies away from the office for lunch. Why don't you join us?"

Harry checked his phone before sliding it into his jacket pocket. "Thank you. My lunch date canceled on me at the last minute and somehow I missed the message."

"If you'd only learn to use the app I installed, this wouldn't keep happening to you," Lies said as he took the chair next to hers.

"I don't know how I'll manage without you." He said it with such a straight face that only she understood he was joking.

Laughter broke out at a table nearby.

Bernard looked at Lies. "Oh? Are you going somewhere?"

"Lies has put in for a transfer," Harry answered for her. He didn't say to where.

"I'd meant to tell you but we got sidetracked," Lies said, silently cursing Harry for giving away a piece of information CSIS hadn't wanted Bernard have. "I'd applied for another temporary position in the Caribbean and it was approved. I leave at the end of next week."

"What an…interesting opportunity for you," Bernard said. "I thought you had your eye on Paris."

"I do. But it isn't going to happen any time soon and I want to see the world. The Caribbean will be fun in the meantime. I like the beach."

Harry ordered a coffee. Even though both men remained civil, the undercurrents of hostility couldn't have proved any more awkward.

"Regretfully, I have another appointment," Bernard finally said. "Lies, it was a pleasure as usual. If I don't see you before you leave, have a safe journey." He patted the pocket with the wire inside it. "Stay in touch."

Lies waited until she was certain he'd left the restaurant before rounding on Harry.

"What is wrong with you?" she demanded. "We were having lunch in public, not clandestine sex in a back alley."

A slow flush built from his collar to turn his neck a brick red. "I really did have a lunch date who canceled. I didn't know you were here. Why can't people make phone calls anymore?"

He hadn't followed her.

And this wasn't disappointment she felt.

The lunch crowd in the restaurant had thinned, leaving them with empty tables on either side of theirs. Harry seemed in no hurry to escape her company, which she took as a good sign that perhaps there was hope yet, or at the very least, they could part on amicable terms. The world was a small place. There was a chance they might cross paths again in the future.

She propped her chin in her hand. "Bernard believes you're stealing business secrets from him and selling them to foreign competitors. He thinks you used Dita and Alcine to collect them, and that you're using me too."

Harry blinked a few times, slowly. "You're making that up."

"I swear it's the truth. And if anyone should feel insulted it's me. He found a wire I'd planted, and instead of thinking a law enforcement agency had finally caught up with him, he jumped to the conclusion that I'm some dim-witted flunky of yours. Congratulations, James Bond. Or should I say Dr. Evil?"

"My God, Lies. You planted a wire in his house? This could have ended so badly. You know he's been linked to the Russian mafia. People connected to him have disappeared."

"You're the one who should be worried," she said. "He

thinks you're encroaching on his turf. That never ends well for the competition."

Harry's shock hadn't faded enough for him to appreciate the warning. "I've never had anyone accuse me of criminal behavior before."

"He's accusing you of doing what he would do. That's how his mind works. Mind you, people are incredibly complex. Do you know he seemed genuinely concerned about me? That was so sweet."

"Adorable," Harry growled.

She stopped baiting him and turned serious. "I know it's difficult to stand back and watch him go free, but sooner or later, Bernard will get what he deserves. Right now he's counting on terrorist organizations being the highest priority for law enforcement agencies worldwide and he's cashing in on it. He's gotten away with too much for too long and he's continually upping the risks. That's the biggest thrill of the game for people like him. Money's the draw, but the thrill is what keeps him invested. Eventually though, if CSIS doesn't tag him with everything we have on him, Interpol, or the CIA, or some other international organization is going to stumble onto the same intel we have and put the pieces together. Canada has its agenda. They'll each have theirs too." And if those Russian mafia connections Harry loved to point out ever decided that Bernard's arrest would be an inconvenience to them, then jail became the least of his worries.

"I don't give a damn about anyone's agenda or what happens to Vanderloord," Harry said. "I want you to be safe."

Flutters tickled the insides of her lungs as the gold flecks in his eyes roamed her face. She couldn't say for certain how he really felt about her, but at least it wasn't indifference. Heat smoldered between them. If she were to salvage anything with him, even if it turned out to be only friendship, now was the time.

"And I wish you'd trust me. I love what I do, and yes, I like the high stakes, but that doesn't make me careless. I was recruited before I finished university. I received the same training as all of my peers. I have a team leader who tracks my progress on cases and helps me assess risks. I'm held accountable for my decisions." She reached for his hand. "You said you don't know me. Spend the weekend with me and I'll prove that you do."

His eyes filled with the temptation to grab what she offered. Reluctance won out. "Sex isn't going to change anything. That's not what I meant when I said I don't know you."

"I know what you meant and it won't be that kind of weekend. Not that I'd say no if you do change your mind, but it would be difficult to pull off at my aunt and uncle's farm. They wouldn't be shocked to discover we're sleeping together. They just wouldn't want to hear any proof of it."

He flipped his palm over and slid his fingers between hers, holding her hand despite the fact they were in public and the room wasn't completely empty of people who might know him as the Canadian trade commissioner.

She took that as a positive sign.

"You'd introduce me to your family?" he asked.

"Yes. Yasmin's parents. If you really want to know everything about me, this is your best chance. All you'd have to do is ask them a question and they'd show me no mercy."

The flutters in her chest became steel-toe-booted kicks. If she'd guessed wrong—if he'd never want her for anything more than a sex partner—his answer would tell her.

The grip on her fingers tightened. "What time should I pick you up tomorrow?"

Harry couldn't find a parking spot outside of Lies's flat on Saturday morning so he called her to meet him on the street.

He didn't know what she had planned. The weekend could turn out to be a new way for her to torture him. But he didn't think so. She genuinely seemed to want to work out a new, and deeper, relationship with him.

He wanted that too. But how long could it last? He was a career diplomat whereas she was a spy. Neither of them was willing to give up their work. There would be no bridging that gaping chasm.

What if she woke up some morning and realized she'd made a mistake?

It had happened to him before. The possibility of a reoccurrence terrified him because it would be different with Lies. He wouldn't walk away as unscathed. Whatever game she had planned, he wasn't playing. Not when he had no hope in hell of winning. The stakes were too high and any advantage was hers.

This weekend was about getting her out of his head.

She appeared at the door, blond curls bouncing. She wore boots, jeans, a heavy wool sweater, and carried a backpack. He'd seen her in various states of dress—and undress—and in different personae. She took his breath in them all.

He got out of the car and confiscated her backpack, stowing it in the trunk while she buckled herself into the passenger seat.

"Onward Jeeves," she said when he joined her, her cheeky tone making him smile in spite of his best intentions not to allow her to affect him.

The drive passed quickly, with none of the awkward stretches of silence he'd prepared himself for. When Lies had something to say she said it, but overall, didn't waste time on meaningless prattle.

She didn't waste it on teasing him either. He missed that more than he liked.

The Wiersma farm had been built in the early 1800s near a little village in Friesland on the outskirts of Bolsward. A narrow road led past a tidy churchyard, over a small bridge, and through a gate. Harry had to stop so Lies could get out and unlatch it, then close it behind the car once he drove through. Beyond the gate, and alongside a narrow canal that cut through a series of fields, stood a windmill, its blades lazily turning. They arrived in time for morning coffee, when the workers took a break and came in from the barns and fields.

The house and the original barn, now a converted machine shed, shared a single roof of clay tiles. Lies's uncle, Elmer Wiersma, met the car as Harry drew into the carport between the house and the garage. He had to be at least six and a half feet tall, all of it muscle from the physical demands of his business. A moment later, her aunt Ola was at the front door.

Harry saw at once that Lies's cousin Yasmin got her coloring from her mother, but took after her father for her height and her looks. Lies, too, looked like Elmer.

There was no doubting how the Wiersmas felt about their Canadian niece. That she was adored became obvious from their wide smiles of welcome, then the curiosity on their faces when Lies introduced him to them.

He shouldn't be here. They were making assumptions

about his place in her life. But he really did want to know more about her and he hadn't been able to resist the lure she'd dangled under his nose.

The front door opened onto a long hall that separated the converted machine shed from the house. They left their bags at the foot of a staircase at the end of the hall and returned to a door that led to a large kitchen and family room. Coffee brewed cheerfully on a pristine countertop. Plants spilled over the broad ledge of the front window. The kitchen table paraded an enormous centerpiece of bright, fresh-cut flowers. A television occupied one wall at the far end of the room. An enormous coffee table, surrounded by eight heavy wooden armchairs with padded seats, swallowed the center of the family room space.

Lies had stopped at the kitchen and was chatting with her aunt in Frisian. Elmer waved Harry through to the armchairs surrounding the coffee table and told him to have a seat.

"So you are Lies's boss?" Elmer asked, squeezing his intimidating frame into one sturdy, padded chair. Blue eyes, fiercer than Lies's, scrutinized Harry. "What do you do?"

The Dutch cared little for status and titles so Harry didn't bother with his. They reserved their respect for hard work. "I facilitate trade between contractors in Canada and the Netherlands."

"And what is Lies's job?"

Lies appeared, carrying two cups of coffee balanced on saucers. She set one on the table in front of Elmer and passed the other to Harry.

"I'm his personal assistant. I do whatever he tells me to," she said, all innocence. "I helped him move a sofa the other night."

Harry had been taking a sip of his coffee and it went down the wrong way. He coughed, clearing his chest.

"She does what you tell her to?" Elmer shot his niece a skeptical look even as he addressed Harry. "Are you certain? Her father always said instructions are suggestions to her. She prefers to do things her own way."

Harry met Lies's eyes. Hers were dancing. He couldn't help but respond to it in kind. "On the contrary. I find she takes direction exceptionally well."

After coffee, Lies and Harry borrowed bicycles from her aunt and uncle and took a tour of the village and surrounding area. She showed him the places she liked most from her childhood visits. She knew quite a few of the local people and had a smile and a word for them all.

She smiled a lot. He'd noticed it before, particularly when she was trying to prod a reaction from him, but had never thought happiness might be a natural and genuine part of her personality. To find that it was lit his insides. A woman who smiled all the time was hard to resist.

They had lunch at a café on a dock next to one of the province's many lakes. A sailboat cruised past on the rippling waters. A hardy windsurfer in a black and red wetsuit braved the cold wind.

"Well?" Lies asked. "You've met my favorite aunt and uncle. Yasmin too. I've shown you where I grew up. What do you think?"

She sounded like a young girl, anxious for approval while pretending not to care how much it meant to her. Her cheeks were flushed a deep pink from the fresh air, bringing out the blue of her eyes, and her blond hair was a jumble. He would have dug his fingers into it and kissed her if they'd been alone. Her vulnerability in this moment touched his heart.

The village was quiet and dull. Her relatives were honest, dependable people—the type he valued too—and it was obvious how much she loved them. She didn't need more excitement around her. Life already crackled from every pore she possessed. She had it to spare.

"I think it suits you," Harry said slowly.

"That's what I've been trying to tell you." She tucked her paper napkin under her plate on the white plastic table so it wouldn't blow away. "I love my work, but when I want to get away from it, when I need to recharge, I either come here or to my family's farm in Ontario so I can relax and be myself."

A light went on in his head. She didn't find him dull. She found him peaceful.

She wasn't playing a game.

He didn't know what to do about it.

At bedtime, Harry carried Lies's backpack and his overnight bag up a steep flight of stairs with risers too small for his feet, giving him the awkward sensation of climbing a precarious ladder while juggling.

They had the second floor of the house to themselves. However, they'd been assigned separate quarters. He dropped Lies's bag in a room at the farthest end of the hall. It had sloped walls and a skylight. His room was closer to the stairs. While smaller than hers, it boasted a sink and mirror for shaving and an extra-long, twin-sized bed.

Lies kissed him goodnight in the hall, which was a disappointment, but they hadn't yet resolved any major issues between them.

He couldn't sleep. Even though the bed's mattress was comfortable the bedsprings creaked every time he rolled over. Not to mention, the thought of Lies only a few doors away left him restless. He missed her presence. The soft scent of her hair. The warm length of her limbs intertwined with his. The gentle sighs she made in her sleep.

Decisions had to be made. They'd both worked hard to get where they were. He could think of no way to mesh their two lives together. Did he let her go?

He had no choice in the matter. She'd be reassigned once she returned to Ottawa. In a few years he'd be transferred and the likelihood of them crossing paths again would further diminish.

The house fell silent except for the various grumblings of a centuries-old building. He'd finally dozed off when the opening and closing of his bedroom door jolted him awake. Lies, clad in a short nightie, darted across the cold room and crawled under the covers with him. He had to wrap an arm around her to keep them both from tumbling onto the floor.

"Your aunt and uncle wouldn't approve," was all he could think of to say.

"They aren't ninety. Do you think they really expect us to sleep in separate rooms?"

Harry contemplated the single bed with its limited capacity. "Yes."

She nestled against him, her hands pinned together between her cheek and his chest. She slid a bare foot up his calf. "Twin beds are all that's available. We can be creative."

"Elmer scares me."

"He's all talk."

"That's easy for you to say. You're trained in hand-to-hand combat and can kill a man with the jab of your finger."

She laughed softly. It rumbled through her body and transferred to his. "I'll teach you how it's done."

"I'd appreciate it."

He played with one of her ringlets, twisting it around his finger and rubbing it with his thumb. She pressed a kiss to the inside of his arm, an inch above the elbow. The gentle, intimate contact sent a stab of pure lust straight to an erection that had been nagging him since nine o'clock that morning when he'd picked her up at her flat. She buffed her thigh against him, causing both pleasure and an exquisite pain.

"I love you," she whispered.

His chest expanded to three times its normal capacity. From the moment he'd met her in John Carmichael's office he'd wanted her. Now she was his and he'd do what he had to—whatever she asked—in order to keep her. To hell with his career.

"I know," he whispered back.

"How very confident of you."

Along with humor, he could practically hear her eyes rolling. "Your aunt gave me one of your baby pictures and your uncle threatened to kill me and hide my body if I ever hurt you. I assumed that isn't their typical welcome for guests—which means I've got to be someone special."

She lifted her head to gaze at him in the semi-darkness. He could feel her eyes on him. "It wasn't hard for them to figure out. I've never brought a man to meet them before."

"No wonder. You'd have to be confident he's not a flight risk. Please tell me your uncle's not the friendliest member of the family. If he is I want you to teach me that lethal finger jab move before I meet your father."

Her palm pressed against his cheek, pivoting his face in line with hers. "Do you want to meet my father?"

"And your mother, grandparents, siblings, pets, neighbors…whoever is important to you. I love you too."

He'd never said those words aloud to another woman. They tripped off his tongue far easier than he'd expected, perhaps because they were so sincere. He did love her. Enough to acknowledge that she could love him even though she was leaving, and trust she'd be back.

Her thoughts had been following the same lines.

"Where do we go from here?" she asked.

"I can search for something in the private sector if it means we'll have more time to spend together."

"Can I make a suggestion?"

"Please do."

She wriggled into a more comfortable position. His drifting fingers made the distracting discovery that she wore no panties beneath her nightie.

Forget about torture. She was trying to kill him.

"Ask John if you can keep me on as your personal assistant. In exchange, you accept postings in countries that are of interest to CSIS and where I can gather intelligence. Between you and John and your connections, you could make that happen."

He tugged his mind off her missing panties and focused on her suggestion. It would give his own work a far different meaning. He wasn't certain if such an arrangement would be good or bad for him, but he liked the idea far more than he would have expected considering how tired intrigue made him and how much he hated the dangerous games Lies enjoyed playing.

But he loved her and wanted her to be happy. She was never going to give up what was important to her. Including him.

And she wasn't going to ask him to give up anything either.

The fact that she also loved him filled him with awe. She was beautiful, clever, brave, and dedicated. How had he ever gotten so lucky?

Because he'd taken a risk.

For her, he'd take more.

"Marry me," he said.

"Someday." The bed groaned under their combined weight as she moved to sit on top of him, her knees digging into his hips as she carefully balanced. "But we've got to get our stages in the right order. Let's concentrate on building our relationship and planning our future. Once we've got those stages settled, we can work on trust and stability."

"I trust you." He hadn't trusted himself. She was right to refuse to marry him. He still had to prove himself to her, although he doubted if that was what she meant. She knew what she wanted.

So did he. Finally.

He was willing to wait for some things but not others. He smoothed his palms up her thighs to caress the bare buttocks straddling him. "How quiet do you think we can be?"

"Given past experience with you and judging by these bedsprings? Not quiet enough." She leaned forward and kissed him, the dark room a cocoon of intimacy around them. Her mouth hovered above his, her breath teasing his lips. "Do you want me to go back to my own bed?"

Never.

He'd talk to John. Between them, they'd pull a few strings. Then Lies, who'd shaken his world from the first moment he met her, could continue to turn it upside down.

He planned to enjoy every minute.

EPILOGUE

THE SHINY, PLAIN GOLD band on Lies's ring finger drew Harry's attention from across the crowded room. He'd never grow tired of seeing it there or stop appreciating what it had gained him. After three years of pulling strings and planning vacations together, never knowing how long they'd be in the same place, he'd finally convinced her to marry him.

He'd placed that ring on her finger less than a week before their departure from Ottawa for Astana, Kazakhstan, where he was the northern Central Asian country's newly minted Canadian ambassador. He and Lies had arrived in its capital city a day before the first major snowstorm of the season. He'd accepted this posting for her work, not his.

Espionage still created some issues between them. In the spring of the past year he'd gotten word from an old friend in the Netherlands that Bernard Vanderloord had been found dead in his Amsterdam home, cause unknown. It had been mentioned to him in passing, a piece of gossip based on a shared acquaintance with the deceased. He hadn't asked Lies if she knew anything about it or if Canada was somehow involved.

Some things were best left alone and he'd learned to let go.

He chose to believe karma had caught up with Vanderloord.

In contrast to the impressively bitter temperatures that had settled over Astana, the people here were warm and welcoming. The party the Canadian embassy was hosting tonight for local staff and their families was designed to help ease their way into Astana society. They'd been warned that even very young children were almost always included in social functions, so Lies had brought an assortment of Canadian candies to distribute as small party favors.

Her Russian, the local language of business, was progressing much faster than his. Right now she had a wide-eyed toddler on her hip and was also trying out a few words in Kazakh on him, much to the amusement of the child's mother. She looked very beautiful and elegant, but in the wholesome, approachable way of the Dutch. The sleek, silver dress she wore fell to the toes of her matching high heels. The tangle of short blond ringlets she couldn't seem to keep under control fascinated the child in her arms, far more so than her mangled attempt to converse.

Harry had finally talked her into marriage, but not yet convinced her it was time to start a family. Maybe the value the Kazakhs placed on it would have some influence. He was thirty-nine years old. She was thirty-one. He'd give it another year or so, and if she still refused to be swayed, he'd let the matter drop. She was enough for him. Children, although nice, weren't a necessity. Her cousin Yasmin had two already, and while Lies adored them, she said she preferred handing them back to their mother.

He dragged his attention away from his bride. Roman Bayzhanov, his eager young translator, had said something to him. It was his son whom Lies was trying to charm.

"Your wife is very eager to explore the country," Roman repeated, more slowly. His English, while good, was heavily accented and he must have thought Harry hadn't understood him. "I've advised her it's best to enjoy city life until the warm weather returns."

Harry had to admire her dedication. She'd wasted no time. Since Canada had gone into serious trade business with Kazakhstan, the Prime Minister's Office was interested in tracking Kazakhstan's progress toward achieving international human rights standards. Her task was to meet with women from all levels of Kazakh society and gather the required information. She'd also provide her opinions and recommendations regarding the status and education of Kazakh women, and if Canada could—or should—offer support.

She'd conducted similar research in other countries he'd been posted to over the past few years, and with impressive and eye-opening results. He predicted that within the next decade she'd be working for the United Nations fulltime as an advocate of international women's rights.

He could hardly wait. There'd be a measure of safety in such a position that currently didn't exist. He'd never like that she sometimes risked her life, but had come to accept and even admire her unwavering dedication to a worthy cause.

She passed the child back to his mother.

Harry excused himself and went to her side. He slid an arm around her waist and whispered in her ear. "We're still on our honeymoon, Mrs. Jordan. Another half hour, then we're out of here."

Her cheeks flushed with color, although not from embarrassment. She hadn't taken his surname. Calling her *Mrs. Jordan* was code for what would follow later, when they were in bed and alone.

"Have I told you yet tonight how much I love you?" she asked.

"I can't remember," Harry lied. "You should tell me again."

He'd never grow tired of hearing her say it, or saying it back. He'd once been so certain he'd wanted nothing to do with intrigue or spies. To be truthful, he didn't. He'd be thrilled if—when—the UN made that call and Lies put CSIS behind her. Until then, she remained an intelligence officer masquerading as an embassy personal assistant.

And his spy at night.

THE END

NOTE TO READERS

Thank you for choosing *His Spy at Night,* the third book in my *Spy Games* series. I hope you loved Harry and Lies. (Wow. Wasn't her name appropriate? I swear I didn't plan it.)

My usual disclaimer:

Canada prides itself on its freedom of information policies and public disclosure, and CSIS, Canada's spy agency, isn't exempt. If you read the actual *Canadian Security Intelligence Act,* however, you'll note there's a great deal of ambiguity to their mandate, and my characters have chosen to exploit it. They are spies, after all.

Next up is Dan and Alycia's story in *Her Spy at Dawn.* I really didn't start off with a story in mind for Dan in this series, but by the time I'd finished writing *Her Spy to Hold,* the second *Spy Games* book, I knew he was going to have one. Poor Dan…

We're going to be seeing a lot more of him in the upcoming *Spy Games* books.

I'll just leave it at that.

Acknowledgments

I have some amazing author friends whose books you should check out. Samanthe Beck, Roxanne Snopek, Robin Bielman, and Hayson Manning all contribute to my work in one way or another. Blame Roxanne and Guinness if storylines take weird turns. It's Robin's fault if the characters end up in jail. In fact, it's her fault if anyone ends up in jail.

And of course, a special thanks to Annette Gallant for being my first reader and a great friend. Keep your eye out for her name in the future. Her books are coming. She promised.

About the Author

Paula Altenburg lives in rural Nova Scotia, Canada, with her husband and two sons. Once a manager in the aerospace industry, she now enjoys working from home and writing fulltime.

Visit her at www.paulaaltenburg.com to view more of her work and to sign up for her newsletter.

You can also follow her on Twitter @PaulaAltenburg and friend her on Facebook:
https://www.facebook.com/PaulaAltenburgAuthor/.

OTHER CONTEMPORARY ROMANCE
TITLES BY
PAULA ALTENBURG

Spy Games series:
Her Spy to Have – Book One, available now
Her Spy to Hold – Book Two, available now
His Spy at Night – Book Three, available now
Her Spy at Dawn – Book Four, coming February 2017

Broken Hearts series:
I'll Love You Forever – Book One, available now
Book Two – TBA
Book Three – TBA

From Tule Publishing:
Her Montana Love

From Entangled Publishing:
Her Secret, His Surprise
Desire by Design

Read on for excerpts from *Her Spy to Have*, Garrett and
Isabelle's story in Book One, and *Her Spy to Hold*, Kale
and Irina's story in Book Two.

Excerpt from

HER SPY TO HAVE
GARRETT AND ISABELLE'S STORY

by Paula Altenburg

"WHY DO YOU DO this?" she asked.

"Do what?"

"Follow me around. Look at me as if you find me fascinating. Touch me, and say nice things to me. And then, you pull away as if you did nothing at all." She gave him a self-deprecating smile. "I've already agreed to tell you everything I know. There's no need for these games."

He didn't deny it, as she'd expected him to. He didn't look sorry for it, either. He raked fingers through his sun-streaked hair, spiking it in the front. He looked like an older version of Kiefer, but much sexier.

And far more dangerous to her peace of mind.

"I do it because I can't help it," he confessed. His eyes glittered. "You seem to bring out the worst in me."

She could say the same about what he did to her. She'd never had a problem with insecurity, or of second-guessing herself, before he came along. All she could do was continue to pretend that he didn't affect her. That her heart didn't race when he looked at her that way.

"Do your worst, then," she said. "One of these days

I'm going to call you on it."

His voice dropped, developing a seductive edge to it that sent a frisson of awareness through her body. "You don't want to do that."

She clenched her fingers more tightly together. "No?"

"Absolutely not." He reached for the door, popping it open. "You might discover I'm not bluffing."

"Wait a moment."

He paused, half turning, one foot already on the ground. Amusement—and something more—lit his eyes as they met hers. "You're calling me on it already?"

Excerpt from

HER SPY TO HOLD
KALE AND IRINA'S STORY

by Paula Altenburg

IRINA WAS COOKING DINNER when the knock came on her kitchen door.

She froze with the steel butcher knife she'd been using to chop green onions for an omelet suspended in midair. She wasn't expecting visitors.

She laid the knife on the wooden cutting block, then crossed the kitchen to the two-panel steel side door of her bungalow, the one that led to her carport, and peered through the curtain. All of her doors and windows were locked. The air conditioning took care of the summer heat and humidity.

Thor stood on her doorstep, hulking and blond, and scary.

He wore his hair in a man bun. The wide smile on his lips and the ridiculous courier uniform did nothing to offset the alarming effect of the shiny black eye and the darkening bruise on his forehead.

Adrenaline kicked her heartrate into high gear. She left the chain in place on the inner door, opening it only far enough so she could speak through the crack. The locked screen door added another layer of protection. It wouldn't stop him if he tried to force his way in, but it would slow him down enough for her to slam the inner door shut and shoot the deadbolt.

"You must have the wrong address. I'm not expecting a delivery."

"Dr. Irina Glasov? My name is Kale Martin. Detective Buchanan suggested I pay you a visit. He said you'd asked for a meeting." He fumbled in his shirt pocket for a piece of ID. He flipped it open and held it up.

She couldn't get a close enough look at it through the screen, not that it mattered. She'd never be able to confirm the legitimacy of it even if she did. Hope warred with suspicion. "Do you mind waiting a few minutes while I give Detective Buchanan a call to confirm it with him?"

The giant didn't take offense to her caution. "Not at all."

She left him on the doorstep while she dug her cell phone and the business card Detective Buchanan had given her out of her purse. She punched in the number.

As it turned out, the detective had, indeed, asked Mr. Martin to stop by. The description he gave her matched the man at the door, right down to the black eye, courier uniform, and running shoes, but Irina continued to hesitate even after she disconnected the call. While this seemed a little elaborate for a hoax, whoever had managed to hack into her computer wasn't trying to be subtle. The implicit threat had been frightening.

She wished she were taller and more assertive. A self-defense course wouldn't have been remiss, either. She'd let Mr. Martin in, but she'd stand at the counter so she'd have the butcher knife close at hand. She'd never be able to use it on anyone, but he didn't need to know that.

She slid back the chain and unlocked the screen door. She didn't open it but retreated to the counter, leaving him to let himself in.

The Norse god stepped over the threshold, his sheer size swallowing what she'd considered a spacious kitchen. If he lifted his hand above his head he could plant his palm on the ceiling. Fine gold hairs sprinkled tanned calves and forearms. Bulging biceps and broad pectoral muscles strained the seams of the gray cotton, short-sleeved shirt. Faint blond scruff, caught in the light from the bay window, stubbled his jaw.

The guy was beautiful. She had a difficult time believing he was an intelligence officer. Weren't they supposed to blend in?

The only place he'd go unnoticed was Asgard.

www.ingramcontent.com/pod-product-compliance
Lightning Source LLC
Chambersburg PA
CBHW051243250626
47155CB00009B/3142